Stories
and In

C000089237

EDGAR ALLAN POE

Simplified by Michael West and Roland John

Illustrated by Christine Tacq

1500 word vocabulary

LONGMAN

R. Mardon.

LONGMAN GROUP LIMITED
London

*Associated companies, branches and
representatives throughout the world*

This edition © Longman Group Limited 1975

This edition first published 1975
New impression 1978

ISBN 0 582 53471 2

Printed in Hong Kong by
Yu Luen Offset Printing Factory Ltd.

Contents

The searchers found a black silk waistcoat

I

'YOU ARE THE MAN'

The miracle of Rattleborough really changed the lives of people in that small town. They certainly pray a lot more than they used to. And so the miracle – whether it was right or wrong – has had an excellent result. I am the only person who knows the whole story of the event; and I am, therefore, the only person who can tell the story properly.

The events happened in the summer of 18— . Mr Barnabas Shuttleworthy had lived in Rattleborough for many years. He was one of the town's wealthiest and most respectable old gentlemen. One Saturday morning, he set out on horseback for the city of P— , fifteen miles away, planning to return the same evening.

Two hours later, the horse returned without Mr Shuttleworthy – and without the two bags which it had been carrying. The horse was wounded in the chest and covered with mud.

Very naturally, these unpleasant facts caused alarm in the town. And when, by early Sunday morning, the old gentleman had still not returned, his friends decided to look for him.

The man who at last decided to lead the search was, of course, Mr Shuttleworthy's closest friend, Mr Charles Goodfellow. 'Old Charley Goodfellow', as everyone called him, was indeed a good fellow. He had an honest, pleasant face, a kind heart, a clear voice and a pair of bright eyes that were never afraid to look straight into anyone's face. Old Charley had nothing to hide.

Although Mr Goodfellow had lived in Rattleborough for only six or seven months, he was very popular with everyone. His name helped, of course, but apart from that, everyone respected him. Mr Shuttleworthy especially liked him, and as the two old gentlemen were next-door neighbours, they had quickly become almost as close as two brothers.

Old Charley was not at all a rich man, and so he had to be rather careful with his money. Perhaps that was partly why Mr Shuttleworthy invited him to meals so often. Mr Goodfellow was at his friend's house three or four times a day, and always at midday for dinner. And then – the amount of wine that the two old gentlemen drank was really nobody's business but their own! Old Charley's favourite wine was *Château Margaux*. Mr Shuttleworthy liked nothing better than to see his friend swallow it, as he did, glass after glass.

I was with them one day, just after dinner, when the Château Margaux had been flowing freely for an hour or more.

'I'll tell you something, Charley,' Mr Shuttleworthy said, hitting his friend on the back. 'You are the finest old fellow I've ever met! And since you enjoy this wine so much, I'll order a big case of it for you. Yes, sir, I'll send an order this afternoon for a double-size case of Château Margaux, the best on the market! I *will* – now don't say a word! I've decided, and that's the end of the matter. So look out for it. It may take a month or two, but it'll come . . . It'll come when you don't expect it.'

This generosity of the rich Mr Shuttleworthy towards his not-so-rich friend shows just how close the two men were.

Well, on that fateful Sunday morning, when Mr Shuttleworthy did not return, Old Charley Goodfellow was the most anxious man in Rattleborough. He looked as pale as death and could not stop shaking, just as if the missing man had been his own dear brother. He knew, of course, that the horse had come home alone – and without its master's two bags. He knew, too, that a pistol-shot had passed straight through the horse's chest, entering at one side and coming out at the other, but not quite killing the poor animal.

At first, Old Charley's grief was too much for him. He could not do anything or decide anything. All he could say was, 'Wait . . . We must wait – until tomorrow, or Tuesday perhaps. He will come . . . '

It is often like that, with people who have to bear some great sorrow. They do not want to do anything – except wait. Well, the people of Rattleborough rather agreed with Old Charley. They would wait for a day or two and see what happened. They would have waited for a week, probably, if Mr Shuttleworthy's nephew had not strongly disagreed.

This nephew, young Mr Pennifeather, was the missing man's only living relation. He had lived with the rich Mr Shuttleworthy for many years. But he was not a very nice man. He played cards for money, he drank too much, he liked to quarrel. If he had not been Mr Shuttleworthy's nephew, no one would have listened to him. But the town had to listen, and agree, when Mr Pennifeather demanded a search for his uncle's '*dead body*'.

Although Mr Goodfellow still seemed unwilling, most people were getting anxious. It was hard for Old Charley to fight against it, and at last he agreed to the search.

'But how do you know that your uncle is dead, sir?' Old Charley asked Mr Pennifeather. 'You seem to know a lot.'

'Yes, how *does* he know?' other people whispered.

When Mr Pennifeather did not answer, there were more angry words between him and Old Charley. The crowd did not take much notice of the quarrel. Everyone knew that the two men were not good friends. Mr Pennifeather, who had very few friends, had never liked Old Charley's close friendship with his uncle, and once, during a quarrel, Mr Pennifeather had knocked Old Charley down. But Old Charley had behaved very well at the time. He had got up from the floor and rubbed the dirt off his clothes. Then he had just said that he would 'remember the matter and deal with it later'. Everyone thought that that was a calm and very proper reply to the young fellow. And no doubt Old Charley, who could never remain angry for long, had soon forgotten the quarrel.

But I must go on with the story. After the discussion, then, Mr Pennifeather advised that the searchers should spread out over the country. The fields and woods between Rattleborough and the city extended for nearly fifteen miles. 'We should spread ourselves out,' Mr Pennifeather said, 'so as to search everywhere.'

Now perhaps Old Charley was growing jealous of Pennifeather. Or perhaps he really was a great deal wiser than the young man. In his clear, honest voice, Old Charley said, 'There's no need for that at all. Mr Shuttleworthy was riding along the road to P— . Why ever should he have left the road? We must look closely on both sides, especially among bushes and trees and tall grass. Don't you think that's the best plan?'

Most of the crowd did think so, and so they all left
Rattleborough together, with Old Charley leading the
way. And a very good leader he was. Although they did
not go far from the road, Old Charley led them into
many dark corners and along unknown paths. But they
did not find Mr Shuttleworthy that day. They went out
again on Monday, Tuesday and Wednesday – still
without much luck.

I mean that they did not find Mr Shuttleworthy or his
body, but they did find some traces of a struggle. They
were following the tracks of the gentleman's horse, and
had reached a spot about four miles east of Rattleborough.
There, a path left the road and ran through a wood. But
it came out again and met the road on the other side of
the wood. A traveller going that way would save half a
mile or more of his journey.

Mr Shuttleworthy clearly had gone that way, as the
horse's tracks showed. Following them along the lane,
the searchers came to a pool of dirty water, and there they
saw the marks of a struggle. Something big and heavy –
much bigger and heavier than a man – had been pulled
off the path into the water. With ropes and chains, the
men searched the pool thoroughly but found nothing.

They had almost decided to leave the place when Mr
Goodfellow said: 'Perhaps we ought to draw off most of
the water.'

Old Charley really had plenty of sense, and as several
men had brought tools, his idea seemed a good one.
Ditches were dug from both sides of the pool, and the
water then ran off along the path.

At the bottom of the pool, the searchers found a black
silk waistcoat. Nearly everyone present knew that it was
Mr Pennifeather's waistcoat, although it was torn and
marked with some dark red colour. Two or three people

remembered that Mr Pennifeather had last worn the waistcoat on Saturday morning – the morning when his uncle had ridden off to P— . No one had seen it since that morning.

The matter looked serious for Mr Pennifeather, and the man could not say a word. His face had turned very pale. The two or three friends that he had moved quickly away from him. But Mr Goodfellow went and stood beside him.

'We must not make up our minds too quickly,' he said. 'You all know that I have forgiven Mr Pennifeather for – for his attack on me a few months ago. Yes, indeed, I have forgiven him from the bottom of my heart. No doubt he can explain this – this unpleasant discovery. And I, certainly, will try to help him. He is my best friend's nephew – poor Mr Shuttleworthy's only relation. For the sake of his uncle, I – I must try to help him.'

Old Charley talked for half an hour. His kindness, his goodness, his honesty seemed to shine through every word he said. But Old Charley was not a clever man. Half his words did more harm than good to Mr Pennifeather. This was especially noticed when Old Charley said the word 'heir'. Instead of saying 'Mr Pennifeather', he said 'the nephew and heir of the good Mr Shuttleworthy'. Once, he even said ' . . . the only heir to the old gentleman's wealth'.

The honest people of Rattleborough had not thought of that before. Suppose that Mr Shuttleworthy was dead: then, if Mr Pennifeather was the only heir, he would get all the dead man's money! Things began to look black for Mr Pennifeather. So, without wasting more time, the crowd tied him up and started back towards the town.

On the way, the searchers looked carefully among the bushes and in the ditches. At one spot Old Charley seemed to pick up something off the ground. Though he tried to hide it, by pushing it into his pocket, a few men saw him. They demanded to know what he had found, and Old Charley had to show it.

It was a Spanish knife – the only one of that kind in Rattleborough. Everyone knew that it belonged to Mr Pennifeather. Indeed, his initials, *D.P.*, were cut into the steel.

No one now had any doubts. Mr Pennifeather had murdered his uncle – so as to get the old gentleman's money. No one troubled to search any more. An hour later, Mr Pennifeather appeared before a judge in Rattleborough Court. It was not a trial, of course, but the judge had to ask some questions.

The judge's first question was: 'Where were you, Mr Pennifeather, on the morning when your uncle disappeared?'

To everyone's surprise, Mr Pennifeather answered, 'I was hunting in the wood.'

'With a gun?'

'Yes, my own gun.'

'In which wood were you hunting?'

'Just a few miles along the road to P— . . . '

Mr Pennifeather had been quite near to the pool where his own waistcoat was discovered! The judge then asked Mr Goodfellow to describe the finding of the waistcoat and the knife.

With tears in his eyes, Old Charley told the story. And after that, he said that he had a solemn duty – not only to God but also to his fellow-men – to tell the truth.

'I have forgiven Mr Pennifeather,' he said, 'for the harm that he once did to me. I now have only the kindest feelings for him. But if this court wants the truth, then I had better tell it. It will – it will – ' Old Charley had to put a handkerchief to his eyes ' – break my heart!'

After a moment, he was able to go on. 'Last Friday I had dinner, as usual, with Mr Shuttleworthy. Mr Pennifeather was with us. The old gentleman told his nephew that he was going to P— the next morning. He intended to take a large amount of money, in two leather bags, to the Farmers' Bank there. Then Mr Shuttleworthy said clearly – and I clearly heard – "Nephew," he said, "when I die, you will get none of my money! Do you hear? None, sir! I am going to write a new will."

'Mr Pennifeather knows very well that that is the truth,' Old Charley added. 'And he must say so!'

Again, to everyone's surprise, the young man's answer was: 'Yes. That is true.'

While the court was sitting, the judge received a message: Mr Shuttleworthy's horse had just died from its wound. Mr Goodfellow thought it would be wise to examine the horse's body.

The judge and the crowd then left the court-house. Mr Goodfellow, who knew a lot about horses, carefully examined the animal's chest. After a long search in the wound, he found the shot which had killed the poor beast. It was a very large shot – the kind that is used for shooting big animals.

The police collected all the heavy guns in Rattleborough and tested the shot in each of them. They found that the shot was too big for all the guns – except one. It exactly fitted the gun of Mr Pennifeather.

The judge at once decided that he had heard enough. He ordered Mr Pennifeather to be kept in prison until the date of his proper trial for murder.

Mr Goodfellow, in tears, begged for the young man's freedom. 'It will be unpleasant,' he said, 'if he has to stay in prison for a month or six weeks. You can depend upon me, sir. I will look after him.'

The judge refused to agree. 'Mr Pennifeather may be guilty of murder,' he said. 'I cannot allow such a man to walk about in the streets of Rattleborough.'

Well, a month later, Mr Pennifeather was brought to trial in the city of P—. The chain of terrible facts was so unbroken and so clear that the result surprised no one. 'Guilty of murder,' the court said. And soon afterwards, the judge read the solemn words: 'You will be hanged by the neck until you are dead.'

The unhappy young man returned to the prison in P—, to wait for his punishment.

Through all this trouble, the noble behaviour of Old Charley Goodfellow had shone like a bright light. The people of Rattleborough loved and respected him even more than before. He was a popular visitor to every house in the town. He had dinner and supper with a different family almost every day. As a result of all this kindness, Old Charley could afford to spend a little money himself. He began to give little parties at his own house, and very pleasant parties they were, too. There were, of course, a few sad thoughts about Mr Shuttleworthy. People also remembered, sometimes, the terrible fate for which Mr Pennifeather was still waiting. But these thoughts did not spoil the occasions.

One fine day, Old Charley was surprised and pleased

to get this letter:

> *To* Mr Charles Goodfellow,   City of W— ,
> Rattleborough.   June 21, 18— .
>
> Dear Sir,
> About two months ago, we received an order from our good friend, Mr Barnabas Shuttleworthy. He asked us to send you a double case of best Château Margaux.
>
> We are pleased to say that we have sent the wine today, by carriage. It should reach you the day after you receive this letter.
>
> Please give our best wishes to Mr Shuttleworthy. We are, sir, always at your service,
>
>   Yours faithfully,
>   Hoggs, Frogs, Bogs, and Company
>   Chât. Marg.
>   6 Dozen Bottles.

Since the death of Mr Shuttleworthy, Old Charley had given up hope of ever getting the wine. He thought of it now – after all the trouble – as a special gift from God. He was delighted, of course. He went immediately to his friends, asking them all to come to supper the next evening. But he did not say anything about Mr Shuttleworthy's present. He just said that he himself had ordered some very fine wine from the city, and that it would arrive the next day. He would be glad if his friends helped him to drink it.

And so, at six o'clock the next evening, a large and respectable company met at Mr Goodfellow's house. I was among them. The supper itself was excellent, and we all enjoyed it. But the Château Margaux did not arrive until nearly eight o'clock. When it came, we decided to put the huge wooden case on the table and open it. I myself helped to lift the box off the floor.

Old Charley had provided other wines for the party, and by eight o'clock he had drunk enough for any man. His face was very red when he sat down then and called loudly for silence. 'Everyone must be quiet,' he cried, 'when we see this great treasure.'

He gave me a few tools and asked me to open the case. Very naturally, I agreed – 'and with the greatest pleasure,' I said. I pushed an iron bar under the cover and hit it gently with a hammer.

The top of the box suddenly flew off. At the same moment, the body of poor Mr Shuttleworthy, covered with blood and dirt, sprang up in the box. It sat there, face to face with Mr Goodfellow, while a smell like poison filled the room. For a moment, the dead eyes looked sadly into Old Charley's face. Then the murdered man's clear but distant voice said slowly – '*You are the man!*' After that, the body fell over the side of the box, on to the table.

I can hardly describe the events that followed. Some people rushed madly to the doors and windows. A few strong men fainted with terror. But after the first wild cries of fear, everyone looked at Mr Goodfellow.

If I live for a thousand years, I will never forget the frightful look on that red, shining face of his. For two minutes, he sat quite still, as if he had been made of stone. His eyes seemed to be looking inwards – at his own miserable, murdering heart. Then they lit up suddenly, and he sprang out of his chair. He fell forward, over the dead body on the table. He began to talk very rapidly. We listened to a complete confession of the murder. Old Charley confessed the whole terrible deed, for which poor Mr Pennifeather was then in prison and waiting to die.

Here are the chief facts of the story that we heard: – Mr Goodfellow had left Rattleborough on his own horse, just behind Mr Shuttleworthy. At the pool in the wood, Old Charley had shot his friend's horse with a pistol. Then, using the pistol as a hammer, he had killed the old gentleman. He took the two bags of money that the horse was carrying.

As the horse seemed to be dead, Old Charley had struggled to pull its body from the pool into the bushes. He had then ridden away, carrying Mr Shuttleworthy's body, to a distant part of the wood. And there, he had hidden the body in a safe place.

Old Charley himself had put the waistcoat, the knife, and the large shot in the places where they were found. In this way, everyone was certain to blame Mr Pennifeather for the murder.

Towards the end of the terrible story, the guilty voice grew weak. Old Charley finished at last, and raised himself from the table. He stretched out his hands to the wall and fell – *dead*.

I have called this event 'the miracle of Rattleborough'. In the minds of the honest people of that town, it *was* a miracle. And it has remained a miracle. Mr Goodfellow's confession came just in time to save Mr Pennifeather's life. But you will want to know, perhaps, how that confession was arranged.

I knew, for certain, that Mr Goodfellow had never forgiven young Pennifeather for knocking him down. I was in Mr Shuttleworthy's house at the time of the quarrel. I saw the look on Old Charley's face when he got up off the floor. And I said to myself, 'That man *never* forgives and *never* forgets.' While everybody else saw only Old Charley's kindness and honesty, I was ready to see other things. Especially if he was dealing with Mr Pennifeather!

In this mystery, Old Charley made most of the discoveries himself. And the strangest one, surely, was his discovery of the shot. If you remember, he found it in the chest of the dead horse. The good people of Rattleborough⋅ had forgotten the facts about the horse's wound! But I had not forgotten them. A pistol-shot had passed *through* the animal's chest. There were, in fact, *two* wounds – one where the shot had entered the body, and one from which it had left. Old Charley must have put that large shot into the wound before he 'found' it there!

I then thought of Mr Goodfellow's pleasant little parties, where there was always plenty of good food and drink. It seemed strange that these had started only *after* Mr Shuttleworthy – and his money – had disappeared.

I made a secret search, lasting nearly two weeks, for Mr Shuttleworthy's body. Of course, I looked in places far from those to which Old Charley had led the searchers. And at last, I found the body. It was at the bottom of an old, dry well – about three miles from the pool in the wood.

The rest of my plan was quite simple. I had not forgotten Mr Shuttleworthy's promise to Old Charley, about the Château Margaux. And so, one night, I brought the old gentleman's body to an empty hut in my garden.

I got a piece of strong spring-steel, about a foot long, and pushed it down the throat of the dead man. I then put the body into an old wine box. I doubled the body over, so that the spring-steel was also doubled. I had to sit on the cover to hold it down, while I was hammering in a few nails. I had no doubt what would happen: the cover would fly off as soon as someone tried to open it – and the body would spring up.

I addressed the box to Mr Charles Goodfellow, Rattleborough, and I also wrote the letter 'from the wine merchants'. My servant was ordered to deliver the box at eight o'clock on the evening of Old Charley's supperparty.

The voice that spoke the words '*You are the man!*' was my own. I had been practising them for several days, and could then imitate Mr Shuttleworthy very well. The general terror in the room was a great help to me, and I also depended upon Old Charley's fear. I was not surprised when he confessed the deed, though I had not expected his death.

Mr Pennifeather came back to Rattleborough – a free man – the next day. He received all his uncle's money, for Mr Shuttleworthy had never written a new will! The young man had gained something from his terrible experience: his habits changed, and he lived happily ever after.

2

THE GOLD BUG

The word 'bug' means an *insect*.

My friend William Legrand lived on a small island, nine miles from Charleston in America. He was a clever man, and he had once been rich. But now he was poor, and this change in his fortune had made him strange.

Sometimes he was sad and silent, and seemed to hate everybody. At other times he was very happy – and most interesting to talk to.

He lived in a hut, with an old African servant called Jupiter, and a big dog. He used to shoot birds and catch fish, and he was a great collector. His collection of shells was the best that I had ever seen. He was also very interested in all kinds of insects.

I went to visit him in late October one year. He was not in his hut. It was a cold day, and so I went in and sat down by the fire. After about an hour, he and Jupiter returned.

Legrand said, 'I'm sorry that I wasn't here to meet you. I found a wonderful thing on the shore today. It's a gold bug – an insect which looks exactly as if it was made of gold. I don't think that a bug like it has ever been found before.'

I said, 'Let me see it, then.'

He answered, 'I met my friend Martin on the way back. He wanted to study it, and so I let him take it. You shall see it the next time you come here. But I will draw a picture of it for you.'

Legrand sat down at a small table by the window and looked for some paper. He could not find any at first but then began to feel in his pockets. 'Oh, this will do,' he said, and took out a piece of dirty parchment. He drew something on the parchment and brought it to me by the fire.

Just at that moment, Legrand's dog pushed open the door and rushed into the room. The dog and I were great friends, and for two or three minutes we had to greet each other. When at last I looked at the parchment, I was puzzled.

'This is a funny kind of bug,' I said. 'It looks more

like a death's head – a skull and cross bones. And there are some marks underneath it.'

Legrand laughed. 'A skull!' he cried, without looking at the drawing. Then he said seriously, 'No, no. I couldn't show the colour, of course. But it's a bug, and I have drawn it well enough.'

He had drawn a good skull and cross bones, not an insect. But I was afraid to say more for fear of hurting his feelings. So I walked across to him and gave him the parchment. I thought that he was going to tear it up, but first he looked at it quickly. His face turned red – and then as pale as death. He examined the parchment carefully for several minutes but did not say anything. At last he locked it away in a desk.

After that, I did not see Legrand, or hear from him, for a month. Then, one day, Jupiter came to visit me at my home. He brought a letter from his master:

'Why haven't I seen you for such a long time? I have made a most interesting discovery, and want to tell you about it. Do come at once. Come *this evening*, with Jupiter.

Your friend,
Legrand.'

I felt a little anxious when I saw the look on Jupiter's face. 'How is your master?' I asked.

'He is not well, sir. I don't know what's the matter with him. He never talks – and a few days ago he stayed out, alone, for the whole day. Something is troubling him – '

'What can be troubling him?'

'I think it's the gold bug, sir! I think it bit him when he picked it up. And the bite has made him ill. I'm very glad that I carried it in a piece of paper.'

I decided to go with Jupiter to the island. When we arrived there, my friend looked pale and tired. He was also in a strange, excited state, with a mad look in his eyes.

'Do you remember the gold bug that I found?' he cried. 'Well, it *is* made of gold – and it will make my fortune for me!'

I felt very sorry for him. Was he so ill that his mind had given way? 'How will it do that?' I asked quietly.

Legrand did not answer. He went to a glass case and brought the insect to me. It was dead, of course, but still very beautiful and exactly like gold. It was also a lot heavier than most insects of the same size. But I knew that it was not *made of* gold.

'Legrand,' I said, 'you are unwell, and . . . '

'No!' he cried. 'I am excited but not ill. I want your help.'

'How can I help you?'

'Jupiter and I are going up into the hills this afternoon. I can trust you, and so – will you come with us? We may be very lucky. I don't know. But if we are not, I shall still feel calmer.'

'I am willing to help you,' I said, 'if you promise me something. When we come back from the hills, you must go to bed. And I will bring a doctor to you.'

'Yes, yes, I promise. We must go now, while it is still light.'

We left the hut at half past three, and the dog came with us. Jupiter was carrying a rope and three spades, and

I had two oil-lamps. Legrand took a ball of string, with the gold bug tied at the end of it. He swung the bug to and fro as he walked. It was a sad sight, I thought.

Two hours later, we reached a spot on high ground. There were many bushes around us, and a few trees. Legrand walked straight towards the tallest tree. It was a bigger tree, and more beautiful, than any of the others that I could see.

'Now, Jupiter,' Legrand said, 'can you climb that tree?'

'Yes, sir. How far up shall I go?'

'Climb up to the first branches, and then I'll tell you. Here, take this with you.' He gave Jupiter the ball of string, with the gold bug tied to it.

It was a very old tree, not difficult to climb, and Jupiter was soon sixty feet up. He was holding the first branch.

'That's the first branch,' Legrand shouted. 'Now go higher – until you reach the seventh branch on that side.'

Jupiter went on climbing, and after a few minutes he called down to us. 'I'm sitting on the seventh branch, sir.'

Legrand was very excited. 'Good!' he shouted. 'Climb out along that branch. Go as far as you can. Tell me if you find anything there.'

A moment later, Jupiter cried, 'O-oh-oh! God have mercy on me! What is this?'

'Well, what is it?' Legrand cried, dancing about wildly.

'It's a skull, master! An old white death's head! And it's fixed to the tree with a nail.'

'Now, Jupiter, listen to me carefully, and do exactly as I say. Can you hear me?'

'Yes, sir.'

'Well, then, find the left eye of the skull. Hold the ball of string, and drop the gold bug through the left eye. Then let out the string as far as it will go. Do you understand?'

'Yes, sir. That's very easy. The left eye – yes, I have it. The bug is coming down, master!'

'Yes, we can see it. Good.' The insect, at the end of the string, was shining in the sunset like a little ball of gold.

After a moment, Legrand shouted, 'Let the string go now, Jupiter, and come down from the tree.'

The gold bug fell to the ground and lay there. Legrand pushed a stick into the ground at the exact spot where it fell. He picked up the gold bug and gave me the other end of the string.

'Hold that end against the tree,' he said. 'At the nearest spot to the stick. I will stretch out the string to its full length. See that it is always touching the stick.'

In a moment, the string formed a straight line – from the tree to the stick, and then to a spot about fifty feet away. Legrand marked the new place where the gold bug lay, and made a circle of clear ground around it.

'Now bring the spades, Jupiter,' Legrand said. 'We must dig here.'

We worked for two hours and dug a very deep hole. By the light of the lamps we saw only – soil and stones. Legrand seemed very unhappy, but he refused to give up.

We were resting after lifting out a very big stone, when Legrand suddenly seized Jupiter's hand.

'Jupiter!' he cried. 'You have two eyes in your head – a left eye and a right eye. Now show me – at once – which is your left eye?'

'Oh, master! This – isn't this my left eye?' Jupiter put his finger on his *right* eye.

'Ah, I thought so!' Legrand cried. 'You do not know left and right! You put the gold bug through the right eye

The insect was shining in the sunset

of the skull. Look, man – this is your left eye! We must try again.'

We went back to the tree. Legrand moved the stick a little, just the distance between two eyes. I held the string against the tree again, and Legrand stretched it out to its full length. The gold bug then lay several feet away from the side of our hole.

Legrand marked another circle around that spot, and we again began to dig. We were all so tired that we worked slowly, without talking. We had been digging for about two hours when Legrand's dog suddenly made us stop work. He began to bark loudly, and the next moment he sprang into the hole. He pulled away the soil madly with his front paws. Almost at once we saw a mass of bones – men's bones. There were the remains of two complete bodies.

We cleared away the bones, and under them we found a long knife. Next we saw three or four bright coins shining in the light from our lamps.

'I expect more than that,' Legrand said. 'Let us go deeper.' As soon as he spoke, his spade struck against metal.

It was a thick iron ring, and it was fixed to the top of a wooden chest. We worked like madmen, and the next five minutes were the most exciting in my life. The chest was very big and strong, with six iron rings round it. Six men, then, were intended to carry it. Certainly, we three could not move it more than an inch.

The box was closed by means of two iron bars. Breathless with excitement, we pulled back the bars. The next moment, a huge treasure of gold, silver and jewels almost blinded us with its light.

I cannot describe our feelings. For two minutes, we stood quite still, just looking at that great fortune. Jupiter was the first to move. He pushed both his arms into the chest – covering them, up to the shoulders, with gold.

'And it all comes from the gold bug,' he whispered in wonder. 'All from that little gold bug.'

After we had got over our surprise, we thought about moving the treasure. Legrand said, 'We must take out all the heavy things and hide them in the bushes. I would like to carry everything home before daylight if we can.'

We could not lift the box out of the hole until it was half empty. But, with the help of Jupiter's rope, we got it out at last. Then, leaving the dog to guard the hidden things, we struggled away with the chest. After a very tiring journey, we reached the hut at one o'clock in the morning. We rested there for an hour and had supper.

'Get three strong sacks,' Legrand said to Jupiter. 'It will be easier to carry the rest of the things in sacks.'

We reached the hole again at four o'clock, and soon had the three sacks filled. Though we were, by that time, very tired again, I was not anxious about Legrand. I did not know how he had found the secret of the treasure. But *that*, and not illness, was the cause of his excitement. We got back to the hut with our heavy sacks just as the sun was rising.

After another rest, we had a good look at the treasure. We made three separate heaps on the floor – a heap of coins, a heap of jewels and one of ornaments.

Nearly all the coins were gold, French, Spanish, German and English money. There was no American money at all. With help from Legrand's books, we decided that the value of all this money was not less than four hundred and fifty thousand dollars.

It was not easy to guess the value of the jewels. There were a hundred and ten diamonds, many of which were very large and beautiful. We counted three hundred and ten pearls, all of them perfect; and over two hundred precious stones of other kinds. These jewels, except the pearls perhaps, had been broken from many different ornaments. We found the gold and silver remains of these ornaments among the heavier pieces.

There were nearly two hundred gold finger- and ear-rings, thirty gold chains and eighty-three heavy gold crosses. We found forty-four gold drinking cups and eight silver ones. There was a huge golden wine-bowl – the heaviest thing in the chest. The weight of all these things was more than three hundred and fifty pounds; and we did not weigh the watches. There were a hundred and ninety-seven splendid gold watches: many of them were very old and did not work, but they all contained jewels and had rich cases.

By the evening, Legrand and I had finished our work. We thought that the value of the whole treasure was one and a half million dollars. Later, after we had sold most of the things, we realised our mistakes; for we received more than two million dollars.

'How ever did you know that the treasure was lying there?' I asked.

He came and settled himself comfortably by the fire. Then he said, 'You were here last about a month ago – and I told you about the gold bug. I drew it for you on a piece of parchment.'

'Yes. It looked like a skull and cross bones.'

'When you gave the parchment back to me, I saw the

skull, too. It puzzled me very much, because my drawing was on the other side of the parchment. Before I drew the bug, I had looked on both sides. They were quite plain though rather dirty. Then, five minutes later, the skull and cross bones had appeared.

'That night, after you had gone, I thought about the problem. Jupiter had found the bit of parchment on the sand. It was near the place where we caught the insect. Jupiter was afraid of the creature, and so he carried it in the parchment.

'Just after that, we met Martin, and I gave him the bug. I must have put the parchment in my pocket.

'Now you know the uses of parchment: things that are written on parchment are always important; the material lasts for hundreds of years. You know, too, that pirates use a skull and cross bones on their flags – '

'But you have forgotten something, Legrand,' I said. 'When you made your drawing, there was nothing else on the parchment. How did that skull suddenly appear?'

'Ah, that was the big mystery, but I soon explained it. I remembered what happened that evening. You were sitting here by the fire. I drew the bug for you and gave you the parchment. Then the dog rushed into the room – do you remember? You scratched his head with one hand, holding the parchment with the other. That other hand must have fallen towards the fire.

'When you looked at the parchment, you saw the skull and cross bones. But my drawing was on *the other side*, and you didn't look at that! I guessed that the heat of the fire had made the skull appear.'

'Secret writing?' I asked.

'Yes. There are special kinds of ink for secret writing.

The colour disappears when the ink dries. If you want to make it appear again, you must heat the paper.

'Well, after you had gone, I heated the parchment. The skull and cross bones became quite clear – in the top left-hand corner. In the bottom right-hand corner the figure of a small goat – a *kid* – appeared.'

'There were some other marks, too,' I said, 'in the middle of the parchment.'

'Yes, but they were not clear. When I saw the kid, I immediately thought of *Captain Kidd*. As you know, he was a famous pirate. I don't know whether he could write or not. If he couldn't write, then perhaps he used the kid instead of his name.'

'So, what did you do?'

'First, I washed the parchment carefully in warm water. And, while it was drying, I thought about Captain Kidd. People don't know much about Kidd – '

'He was a very successful pirate,' I said. 'I mean – his evil deeds made him very rich.'

'Yes, but what happened to his treasure? There are stories that he hid it in a secret place along this coast. Hundreds of people have searched for it. There are no stories about anyone *finding* it. If Captain Kidd had hidden his gold, he would have made a note of the place. Then I thought – perhaps he lost the note. We shall never know the truth about that, but – '

'Yes, yes. Go on with your story!' I cried.

'You are as excited as I was that night! Well, when the parchment was dry, I put it in a flat tin. And I heated it over the fire.'

Legrand got up then and brought the piece of parchment from his desk. He laid it in a tin and put the tin on the fire. A few minutes later, he gave me the parchment.

I saw the skull and cross bones, as before. I saw the kid, too. Between them I saw this message:

```
53ZZQ305))6*A4826)4Z.)4Z)A806
*A48Q8X60))85A1Z(A:Z*8Q83(88)
5*QA46(A88*96*?A8)956*2(5*Y4)
8x8*A4069285)A)6Q8)4ZZA1(Z9A4
8081A8:8Z1A48Q85A4)485Q528806
*81(Z9A48A(88A4(Z?34A48)4ZA16
184?*Q(8Q188AZ?A
```

'I don't understand it at all,' I said. 'What does it mean?'

'It isn't very difficult,' Legrand replied, 'because Captain Kidd wasn't a very clever man. After some careful study, I understood it well enough. The first question is important: in what language is the message?

'I decided it was in English – because of the kid, of course. A little goat is a kid only in English. Now each sign in the message stands for an English letter. And the next question is: which sign is used most often? I counted them all and made this list.'

Legrand gave me the list, and I read:

Sign	Times used	Sign	Times used
8	34	1	8
A	22	0	6
4	18	9	5
)	15	3	4
Z	14	2	4

6	‖	?	4
*	‖	:	2
5	10	X	2
Q	9	Y	1
(	9	.	1

'Did this list help you very much?' I asked.

'Oh yes. If you look at any English book, you will find that some letters are used far more often than others. The letter *e* is used very often indeed, but *x* and *z* are hardly used at all. So I thought that Kidd's figure 8 stands for the letter *e* . 8 appears thirty-four times in the message. Double *e* is also common in English, in words like *meet* and *seen*. And there are five 88 signs on the parchment.'

I looked at the parchment again then, but the signs had faded. Legrand went to his desk and brought me a copy of the message. I counted the 88 signs.

Legrand went on: 'After that, I thought about common words. The words *a* and *the* are very common in English. *The* is perhaps more common than *a*. In the message, the signs A48 , in that order, are repeated six times.'

'You are very clever,' I said. 'So A stands for *t*, and the figure 4 means *h*.'

'Yes. And the signs A(88 may be the word *tree*. Towards the end of the message, we see these signs:

A48A(88A4(Z ?34A48

and so we can write:

the/tree/thr---h/the

and we can guess the word *through*.'

I said, 'So Z stands for *o*, ? means *u* and 3 means *g* !'

Legrand then pointed to the end of the second line of the message. 'Here we have the signs Q83(88 , and we know that it means – *e g r e e* . This is clearly the word *degree*. So Q stands for *d*.

'Well, I continued in the same way and guessed many more words. One or two names have changed since Kidd's death, so I had to study some old maps of the coast. And his spelling was not always correct either! But at last I wrote out the message, and here it is.'

Legrand gave me another piece of paper, and I read:

'A good glass in Bessop's Castle in the devil's seat – forty-one degrees – north-east and by north – the main part of the tree – seventh branch on the east side – shoot from the left eye of the skull – a line from the tree through the shot fifty feet out.'

Legrand said, 'The Bessop family used to own a lot of the land in this part of the country. I talked to some of the oldest people here. And at last I met a very old woman who had worked for the Bessops when she was young. She said that the Castle wasn't a real castle – it was a high rock. She offered to take me to it.'

'You were lucky to find her,' I said. 'Did you also find the rock?'

'There were several rocks, but one of them was a lot higher than the others. It looked rather like the tower of a castle. I climbed to the top of it and looked around. I was trying to find something that Kidd might have called "the devil's seat", and at last I found it.

'It was a flat shelf of rock, very narrow, and with a high straight back. It was a few feet below me, and so I slid down and sat in it. There were other rocks on both sides of the seat. And I found that I could see only in one direction. I suddenly understood the secret of the message.

'Kidd's "good glass" was a seaman's glass – a telescope! Perhaps, if I sat in the devil's seat and used a telescope, I would find something. I would need a compass, too, so as to point the telescope in exactly the right direction.'

'Forty-one degrees, north-east and by north,' I said.

'Yes. I was very excited. I hurried home, got my telescope and my compass, and returned to the rock. When I had found the right direction, I looked carefully through the telescope. At last, by moving the glass slowly up and down, I noticed a strange white spot. It was in the centre of an opening, near the top of a tall tree. Though the tree was about a mile away, I thought that the white spot might be a skull.'

'And, of course, it *was*,' I said. 'Did you go to the tree before we all went there together?'

'No, but I marked the spot carefully. I knew that I should be able to find it. It was the tallest tree on all that high ground. I knew that Jupiter would find the skull on the "seventh branch on the east side". Then he had to "shoot", or drop something, through the left eye of the skull to the ground.'

'So you used the gold bug at the end of a string.'

' – And I marked the spot where the insect fell. My string was exactly fifty feet long. It gave us a straight line from the tree and through the place where the insect fell. I thought that Kidd's treasure would be hidden there.'

'Jupiter dropped the bug through the *right* eye,' I said. 'And so we were wasting our strength when we dug the first hole.'

'We were two or three feet away from the treasure. It wasn't far – but it was far enough to be important.'

'Yes. Now there is only one thing that still puzzles me. Whose bones did we find in the hole?'

'We can never be sure,' Legrand replied. 'They were probably the bones of two of Captain Kidd's seamen. Someone must have helped him to hide the treasure. Then he killed them, perhaps. Dead men tell no tales!'

3

THE STOLEN LETTER

One evening, I was with my friend Auguste Dupin at his house in Paris. We were sitting by the fire, enjoying a smoke after dinner, when there was a ring at the door-bell. A moment later, Dupin brought in his friend Georges Godinot, the head of the Paris Police.

'Sit down, Georges,' Dupin said. 'Tell me what you have been doing. I am always interested in your cases.' He added, with a smile, 'The Paris Police never fail, do they?'

The police often asked Dupin to help them; and that was why my friend had smiled.

'Not often,' Georges said. He sat down and began to smoke with us. 'I have come to tell you about a very curious case. It is really quite simple, and no doubt we shall succeed by ourselves. But I thought you would be interested in the facts.'

'It is not a murder, I hope,' said Dupin.

'Oh, no. It's a simple matter, but we are puzzled about it.'

'Ah, it is so simple that it has beaten the police!'

'You make me laugh, Dupin. The facts are secret, of course, but I will tell you. There is a promise of 50,000

francs to the man who finds the thing. If it isn't found,
I may lose my place as head of the police.'

'Go on,' Dupin said.

'Well, the Princess received an important letter written
on good white paper. It came in an envelope which had
the initial of the sender, "*S*", on the back.

'The Princess opened it and was just going to read it
when the Countess Duval came in. The Countess, as you
know, is a great talker: she talks to everyone in Paris and
tells all the news. She is a walking newspaper! The
Princess did not want her to see the letter. So she quickly
put it back in the envelope and laid it on a table.

'Soon after that, Mr Lebrun entered the room. You
know that he is an important man in the government.
He is also an unpleasant man: he will play any kind of
nasty trick if it is likely to succeed.'

'I know him,' Dupin said. 'He is very clever, too.'

'Well, Lebrun saw the envelope on the table, with the
initial "S" upwards, and he probably guessed the lady's
secret. While they were all talking, he took a letter
from his own pocket and opened it. Later, he pretended
to read it. Then he put it down on the table, beside the
Princess's letter.

'The three of them talked for ten minutes longer. At
last, as Lebrun was leaving, he took the Princess's letter
and left his own on the table. The Princess saw all this,
of course, but could not say anything.'

'Why not?' I asked.

Georges answered, 'Because of the Countess. If the
Princess had stopped Lebrun, he would have said: "Oh,
you mean this letter? I *am* sorry. I see that it is from S— "
Then the Countess would have spread the news all over
Paris: "Have you heard? – the Princess has a lover! His
name is S— ". '

Lebrun took a letter from his pocket

Dupin said, 'That was a nasty trick! The Princess knows that Lebrun stole her letter. And he knows that she knows!'

Georges went on: 'The letter has given Lebrun great power over the Princess. He has been using that power – secretly, of course, for two months. The Princess must now always support him in the government.'

'Have you looked for the letter?' Dupin asked.

'My men have searched Lebrun's house very thoroughly. It was not easy because we had to search in secret. But, fortunately, he is very often away at night, and his servants sleep in another house. As you know, I have keys which can open any door in Paris. So we searched the house, room by room, for twenty nights. But we did not find the letter.'

'Well, then,' I said, 'it may not be in the house.'

'It probably *is*,' said Dupin. 'If Lebrun has to use it against the Princess, he might need it very suddenly.'

I said, 'Perhaps he carries it in his pocket.'

Georges replied, 'No. My men, dressed as thieves, attacked him twice. They searched his clothes and took his money. But he wasn't carrying the letter.'

'Your men attacked him!' Dupin cried. 'That was unnecessary, Georges. Lebrun is not a fool. He would expect the police to search him in some way.'

Georges laughed. 'When we catch the "thieves", we shall give the money back to him!'

'Tell me about your search of the house,' Dupin said. 'Where did you look exactly?'

'We looked everywhere, I think. We spent three or four nights in each room. We looked on and under every chair and table; on and inside every desk and bookcase. We took the legs and the tops off the tables.'

'Why did you do that?' Dupin asked.

'To see if the letter was hidden there.'

'We can be sure that Lebrun would not do that,' Dupin said. 'Where else did you look?'

'We have long, steel needles which we push into beds and cushions and other soft things. If anything had been hidden inside, we should have found it. We also examined the walls and the floors of every room.'

'Did you search all Lebrun's clothes?' I asked.

'And his books and papers?' Dupin added.

'We did.'

'Did you examine the garden?'

'There is only a yard,' Georges replied. 'And it is covered with large stones. Grass was growing between the stones; so it was easy to see if a stone had been moved. None of them had been moved.'

'Is there a place under the house where Lebrun keeps wine?'

'We found only a few bottles of wine. It would be difficult to hide a letter inside a bottle. But we looked at all the bottles, full and empty. We found nothing.'

After that long discussion, Dupin did not say anything for several minutes. The three of us just sat in silence and smoked. At last, Georges stood up to go.

'Well, Dupin,' he said, 'what do you advise me to do?'

'To search the house thoroughly again.'

'Is that really necessary?' Georges asked. 'I'm quite sure that the letter is not there.'

'That is my best advice, Georges. You could, of course, ask the government to help you. Lebrun stole that letter, and so he has broken the law.'

'I know that. But the letter is very secret. The Princess does not want anyone to know about it. I am the only person she has told.'

'Can you describe the letter?' Dupin asked.

'Oh, yes.' Georges took a little book from his pocket and read an exact description of the letter and the envelope.

Then Dupin said, 'There are people in Paris who may be able to help you. You know them as well as I do. But you will have to pay them, of course.'

'I'm quite ready to pay,' Georges said. 'I have the 50,000 francs in my pocket all the time. The trouble is – I cannot trust anyone with this secret.'

Georges was in very low spirits when he left us that night. Shortly afterwards, I said good night to Dupin and went home myself.

One evening, about three weeks later, Georges came to Dupin's house again. As before, we were having our usual after-dinner smoke. Georges sat down with us.

After a time I said, 'Well, Georges, what about the stolen letter? Have you found it yet?'

'No. We searched the house again, as Dupin advised. But it was a waste of time.'

'How much did you say that you would pay for the letter?' Dupin asked.

'I'm ready to pay 50,000 francs for it. The matter is growing more important – and more dangerous – every day.'

'Well, then,' Dupin said, 'give me the money, and I will give you the letter.'

Georges's mouth opened wide – and so did mine. Neither of us could say a word. We sat quite still for a minute, looking at Dupin. Then Georges dug his hand into an inside pocket of his coat and drew out a large, thick envelope. Without a word, he gave it to Dupin.

Dupin counted the money carefully. When he was satisfied, he went to his desk, unlocked it, and put the money inside. He took a letter from the desk and gave it to Georges.

'Here is the Princess's letter,' Dupin said.

Georges opened it and, with shaking hands, read the message. He sprang out of his chair and rushed to the door. He left the house without saying a single word.

My friend said, 'The Paris Police are quite clever in the ordinary way. They are careful, and they work hard; and so they usually get good results. They have one unfortunate weakness: they have no imagination.

'They never try to imagine other people's thoughts. They treat all problems in the same way. If a stupid man steals something and hides it, the police nearly always find it. But if the thief is a clever man, the police are in difficulties.'

'You mean,' I said, 'that they always search in the same way – and in the same places.'

'Yes. They search in the legs of tables and inside cushions. A clever thief would not hide a thing in a place like that. He would put it in a place where the police may not look.'

I said, 'But is Lebrun such a clever thief? I'm sure he does not often steal!'

'He doesn't, of course. But I know him quite well, and he is a man – with imagination.'

'Go on,' I said. 'Tell me how you found the letter.'

'First, I thought about Lebrun himself. He is in the government, and he is also important at Court. Such a man knows all about the police. He knew that they would search his house. Perhaps he even stayed away at night on purpose – '

'Why would he do that?' I asked.

'So that they could search in peace! He guessed *where* they would look. He knew that they would examine the furniture and the beds – '

' – The books and the bottles!'

'Every small, dark corner!' Dupin cried. 'Lebrun guessed – correctly – that they would not look in the simplest place. Some things are *too* simple for the police!'

'So what did you do?' I asked eagerly.

'One morning I went to Lebrun's house, and I wore a pair of dark glasses for the occasion. I complained of my weak eyes and asked if he knew a good eye-doctor. While we were talking, I looked carefully around the room.'

'And he did not notice that – because of your dark glasses,' I said.

'Right. He was also looking in his address-book for the address of a doctor he knew. Well, there was a big table near the window, with a lot of papers and letters and several books on it. There were two smaller table, with nothing on them at all, a large bookcase, half a dozen chairs and several pictures. None of these things interested me very much. At last, my eyes rested on the fire place and – ' Dupin stopped then and felt in his pocket.

'Yes? On the fire place – and what?'

'On an ordinary letter-holder beside the fire place. It was hanging by a dirty string from a nail in the wall.'

I lay back in my chair, trying to be calm. Dupin had chosen that moment to take out a cigarette and light it.

'Was there anything in the letter-holder?' I asked.

'There were two or three cards and one letter. The envelope was dirty and torn. I could just see the writing of the address. Of course, the thing looked quite different from the description that Georges gave us. The envelope was a different size, too. But I immediately said to myself, "*That* is the Princess's letter."'

'Do you mean that Lebrun had changed the envelope?'

'Why not? It is very easy to change an envelope. And the *place* would probably deceive the police. Remember – the Princess's letter was secret and important: was Lebrun likely to put it in an ordinary letter-holder?'

I said, 'Georges and his men would not think so!'

'Exactly! And Lebrun might have guessed that – because he is a man with imagination. The letter-holder was the simplest, most natural place for a letter in the house!'

'So Lebrun had not hidden it at all!'

'From the police,' Dupin said, 'he had hidden it very successfully. They never notice a thing just in front of their noses.'

'Did you find some way of taking the letter?' I asked.

'Oh no, not that morning. But when I left Lebrun, I also left my gold cigarette case on the table. That evening, I made one or two arrangements.'

'To get the letter?'

'The next morning, I went back to Lebrun's house for my cigarette case. I talked to him for a few minutes, and then we heard a gun-shot outside in the street. There were cries and the sounds of running feet.

'Lebrun ran to the window, opened it and leaned out. I went to the letter-holder, took out the letter, and put it in my pocket. I put another letter back into the holder – a letter that I had written myself. The two envelopes were exactly the same, dirty and torn, and the writing of the address was the same, too. After that, I went to Lebrun at the window.'

'What was the trouble in the street?' I asked.

'A man had fired an old gun and frightened everybody. But the gun was harmless – it had powder but no shot. The police warned the man and then let him go. I left Lebrun's house then. Half an hour later, I met the man with the gun; and I paid him the hundred francs I had promised.'

'Well, well,' I said, 'that's an interesting story.'

Dupin replied, 'But it is not the end, of course.'

'Why not? What else is there?'

'Lebrun has to be punished, hasn't he? He thinks that he still has the Princess's letter. And so he will go on treating her as if she is in his power. She is not – indeed, he is now in *her* power. So she will soon be able to punish him herself.'

'Yes, yes. I had not thought of that.'

'It will be a terrible punishment – and the end of Lebrun's work for the government. I am almost sorry for him. One day, Mr Lebrun will receive a *little* punishment from me, too. I do not like a man who treats a lady as he has treated the Princess.'

'But how – what can you do, Dupin? The thing must remain a secret.'

'Well, as I said, I put another letter in the holder. Lebrun will have to open it sooner or later.'

'Oh, you wrote a letter, did you?'

'Of course. And I should like to see his face when he reads it.'

'Why? What did you write?'

'Just a line or two:

'A man who shows no honour to a lady
Should expect none from a gentleman.'

4

THE MURDERS IN THE RUE MORGUE

When I was in Paris, I stayed with Auguste Dupin for several months. He was a clever man. He could put facts together and understand their meaning. He had trained himself to see not only the ordinary facts of a case but also the facts that were not ordinary. And so he was able to find the answer to a mystery which other people could not understand.

The murder of two women in the street named Rue Morgue was just such a mystery.

This was the report in an evening newspaper:

About three o'clock this morning, terrible cries were heard from a room at the top of a house in Rue Morgue. It was the house of Madame Espanaye and her daughter Camille.

The front door of the house was locked, but a policeman broke it open, and, with several other men, he ran inside. By that time, the cries had stopped. But as the men rushed up the stairs, they heard two voices shouting angrily. The sounds seemed to come from somewhere at the top of the house.

When the men reached the third floor, these sounds also stopped, and everything was quiet. They ran from room to room. At last they came to a large room at the back of the house. The door of this room was locked, and the key was on the inside. The policeman broke open this door, too.

The room was in terrible disorder. The furniture

Terrible cries were heard from a room at the top of a house

was broken and thrown about. There was one bed: the bedclothes had been thrown into the middle of the floor. Under a chair, the men found a long knife, covered with blood. Two or three handfuls of thick, grey hair lay by the fireplace. The hair had been pulled by the roots from someone's head. There were several gold coins on the floor, a gold earring, and two bags full of money – four thousand francs.

At first, the men could not find either Madame Espanaye or her daughter. But the fireplace was very dirty. Looking up the chimney, the policeman made a terrible discovery: the dead body of the daughter had been pushed out of sight up the chimney. The strength of four men was needed to pull it out.

The body was still warm. There were cuts and scratches on the face and arms, and the deep marks of fingernails around the throat. The neck had been broken.

After searching the whole house, the men went outside to a yard at the back of the house. There they found the body of Madame Espanaye. Her head had been almost cut off with a sharp knife.

At present, the police have no idea who carried out these terrible murders.

Early the next day, Dupin went out to buy the morning papers. We read them while we were having breakfast. This was one account:

The police have questioned many people about the murders in Rue Morgue. The facts are certainly not yet clear.

Pierre Musset of the Paris Police said that people

had called him when they heard cries coming from the house. He broke open the front door and entered the building with other men. By then the cries had stopped. A moment later, they heard two angry voices. One was the deep voice of a man saying *Mon Dieu!* (My God!), *Nom de Dieu!* (Name of God!) and *Diable!* (Devil!).

The other voice was very high. He could not say if it was the voice of a man or woman, but the sounds were not like French.

Henri Duval was one of those who entered the house. He knew Madame Espanaye and her daughter, and had often talked to them. The high voice was not that of either of the dead women. He thought that it was the voice of an Italian. He did not himself speak Italian or know any Italians.

Karl Odenheimer was passing the house when he heard the women's cries. They were loud and long and terrible. The high voice was a man's voice. He believed that it was speaking English. At least, it sounded like English, but he himself could only speak German.

An Englishman, William Bird, also entered the house. He said that the deep voice was that of a Frenchman. The other voice was loud and spoke quickly. It might have been Chinese, though he did not know Chinese and had no Chinese friends.

Alfonzo Garcia, Italian, agreed that the deep voice was that of a Frenchman. The high voice was speaking in Russian – he was quite sure of that. He did not understand the Russian language, but the sounds were certainly Russian.

All these men agreed about the rooms upstairs. The door of the large room was locked on the inside when they reached it. All the windows of the house were also firmly shut on the inside.

Jean Migard, owner of a bank, said that Madame Espanaye kept her money in his bank. Three days before her death, she had taken out four thousand francs. The money was put into two bags and delivered to her house. This was done because the bags were too heavy for the old lady to carry.

Adolphe Lebon worked in Migard's bank. Three days before the murders, he had taken two bags of money to Madame Espanaye at her house. He said, 'I did not go into the house at all. When she opened the door, I put the money into her hands.'

On the last page of the newspapers, there was some late news: the police had taken Lebon away to prison.

Dupin read the papers thoroughly and then turned to me.

'What do you think?' he said. 'We must try to find the right answer to this mystery. Lebon is a friend of mine. I do not believe that he is a murderer. We know Georges Godinot, the head of the Paris Police. He will let us visit the house in Rue Morgue; and we shall also see the bodies.'

'What do *you* think about it, Dupin?'

'It sounds very unusual. I do not think that the police will find the killer – or killers. They do not search in the right way. This is the kind of mystery that may be *too* plain for our friend Georges!'

When Dupin had got permission from the head of the police, we went straight to Rue Morgue. But before going into the house, we walked slowly around it. Dupin carefully examined the walls and windows. At a corner of the house, he picked up something and put it in his pocket.

Inside the building, we went to the room where Camille's body had been found in the chimney. Both bodies were there now, and my friend examined them thoroughly. Everything else was still lying as it had been found.

While Dupin was working, I talked to the policeman with us. Dupin spent a long time at the two windows in the room. He seemed to study everything with the greatest care – the door, the furniture, the fireplace, the chimney, the grey hair on the floor.

At last we left the building. On our way home, Dupin stopped at the office of a newspaper, and went inside. I waited for him in the street. For the rest of the day, he said nothing to me about the murders.

In the morning, too, he was silent about them, even after we had read the papers.

It was midday, I think, when he said to me suddenly: 'Did you notice anything unusual about those killings in Rue Morgue?'

I replied, 'No, I don't think so. The newspapers had told us what to expect there.'

'Yes, but the papers do not help. They only print the things that everyone knows. These killings are quite different from ordinary murders. That is why the answer may not be difficult to find '

'Georges Godinot seemed very puzzled,' I said.

'I have just told you *why* he is puzzled: because these deaths are so *different* from other murders.'

'The voices that were heard puzzled me, too,' I said.

'Didn't the force seem unusual?' Dupin asked. 'The unnecessary force that was used to kill the ladies?'

'And how did the killers escape?'

'That is another difference. No one was found upstairs, except the dead woman. And the only way out of the house is – down the stairs! These facts are not difficulties. They make the case easier. But Georges thinks that they make it more difficult.'

'Well, let us go for a walk, Dupin, and you can tell me about it.'

'No. We must stay here. I am waiting for a man who will tell us about it.'

I looked at my friend with the greatest surprise. 'Do you mean – *the murderer?*'

'He is not guilty of murder – I am sure of that. *He* did not kill the women, but he knows what happened.'

'And – have you asked him to come here?'

'I think he will come. When he comes, we may have to keep him here.'

Dupin went to a desk and took out two small pistols.

'These are loaded,' he said, offering one to me. 'We will keep them in our pockets. I hope that we shall not have to fire them.'

I took the gun from him and put it in my coat pocket. My friend then went on with his explanation. I sat and listened with great respect.

He said, 'I quickly made up my mind about the voices that were heard. Let us say that the deep voice was the voice of a Frenchman. But the other voice – the high voice – must have been very unusual. The policeman could not say whether it was a man's or a woman's voice. Duval thought that it was an Italian voice. Alfonzo Garcia, who *is* Italian, said that the sounds were Russian.'

'Yes, yes. I remember,' I said. 'And the German – what was his name?'

'Odenheimer.'

'Yes – Odenheimer. He said that the voice sounded English.'

'But Bird, an Englishman, disagreed. In his opinion it was Chinese. No one seemed to hear any clear words – only *sounds*. Well, I had almost decided about that voice before we went to the house.

'The next question was: how did the killers escape? One fact was certain: they had escaped from the room where the daughter's body was found.'

I said, 'The door of that room was found locked. And the key was on the *inside* of the door.'

'Correct,' said Dupin. 'If the killers escaped through the door, and locked it after them, the key would not be on the inside. So here is another fact: the killers did *not* escape through the door.'

'They must have got out through a window, then, or through the chimney.'

'Correct again. I looked up the chimney. The lower part of it was wide enough to hold the daughter's body. But the upper part was very narrow. No one, not even a child, could get out through that chimney.'

'So they escaped through one of the windows.'

'That is certain,' Dupin said. 'The police do not believe it – because both windows were shut tight. Georges told me that his men could not open them at all. But the fact is certain: the killer or killers escaped through one of the windows in the large room. There is no other way.'

I said, 'You examined the windows with great care. What did you discover?'

'Care is always necessary. Sometimes the police do not know the facts, because they do not take enough care. The two windows in the room were "sash" windows – you know the kind. There are two parts: the upper half is fixed, but the lower half can be raised to let in air. When the lower half is raised, there must be something to support it. Or it will fall down with its own weight.

'In these windows, there were holes through the wood of both parts – and a long nail. To raise the lower part, the nail must be taken out. Then, when the lower part is up, the nail can be pushed through both holes. And so the nail holds the window open. The police must have seen the nails. They probably decided that both windows were nailed shut. But the fact remained: the killers *had* escaped through a window.'

'So it must be possible,' I said, 'to open at least one of them.'

Dupin went on: 'I stood by the first window and took out the nail. But I could not raise the window. There must be, I thought, a hidden spring to keep it shut. After careful searching, I found the spring and pressed it. There was no need for me to open the window.

'I put the nail back in the hole and considered the matter. "Suppose," I thought, "that the murderer went out through this window. Its own weight would make it shut itself, and the spring would keep it shut. But what about the nail? It was found in the hole. The killer could *not* have put it back there after he had left. So what does that prove?" '

'It proves,' I said, 'that he did not escape through that window. He must have used the other one.'

'Right,' said Dupin. 'Next I examined the second window. The spring was exactly the same as the first one. The nail, too, looked the same – and seemed to be fixed in the same way.'

'That must have puzzled you!'

'Puzzled me? Not at all,' Dupin said. 'I was dealing with facts, not with guesses. The facts had led me to this second window – and its nail. As I said, it *looked* just the same as the first nail. But looks are not facts! This nail was the end of the mystery.

'I said to myself, "There must be something wrong with the nail." I took it out of the hole. It was only half a nail! The rough end of it was quite bright, and its other half, broken off, was still somewhere in the wood. It was certainly not long enough to hold the window up.

'I put it back in the hole, and again it looked like a perfect nail. I pressed the spring and raised the window a little. The nail went up, too!'

'You were right, then,' I said. 'The murderers escaped through that window.'

'Yes – and shut it, with great force, behind them; with enough force, I mean, to break the nail. The spring kept the window shut and deceived the police. Now how did the killers reach the ground? – that is the next question.'

'Well – not down the stairs,' I said. 'There were already people rushing *up* that way.'

'True. They left through the window. And I believe that they had entered the house in the same way. If that window had been held open by the nail –'

'But remember, Dupin – it was high above the ground. Murderers cannot fly through the air!'

'And you remember the facts, sir. They escaped. So they certainly reached the ground. We need only consider – *how* it was done.'

'Tell me, please.'

'They left through a window that is not far from the corner of the house. When I examined the house and yard, I noticed a pipe at the corner. Rain-water from the roof flows down the pipe to the ground. The distance from the pipe to that window is about a metre and a half.'

'A metre and a half! It is too far to reach.'

'I agree. It would be difficult – and dangerous – for a killer to spring from the pipe to the window. But if he was accustomed to such exercise, he might be able to do it. If the window was open, that would help him a lot.'

'He would have to be very brave – or very stupid!'

'Still, it is possible. Try to keep all the facts in your mind. Think of that difficult, dangerous spring from the pipe to the window – and, later, *back*. Think of the unusual voice that was heard, and the terrible *force* that the killer used.'

I thought suddenly that I was beginning to understand Dupin's idea. But he went on talking.

'The police are wasting their time looking for reasons for these murders. I do not believe there are any reasons. Georges is puzzled about the four thousand francs. "Why didn't the killers take the money?" he asked me. "They just left it in the bags on the floor!"'

'Lebon is in prison – just because he delivered the money to Madame Espanaye. But the women were killed three days after they received the money; and the murderer did not want it! We need not consider the money at all. It was just an accident, a curious chance, and nothing more.'

'What was just an accident? I asked, puzzled.

'Well, the two events, don't you see? There was a lot of money in the house – and the women were killed. I mean – they were not killed for the sake of the money.'

'Yes, yes. I agree.'

'The daughter's neck was broken,' Dupin went on, 'and her body was pushed up the chimney. Was there a reason for that? Has any other killer ever tried to hide a body in that way? Handfuls of Madame Espanaye's hair were torn from her head. Her head was then almost cut off – it was the deed of a – of a . . . She must have been already dead when she was thrown out of the window. Did the killer have a reason for that? No, no reason at all.'

'No reason,' I repeated. 'Just blind force, a daring spring, a strange voice . . . '

Dupin got up and went to his desk. He took down a book from a shelf above the desk. An envelope was pushed in between the pages of the book.

'When I saw the daughter's body,' he said, 'I knew the kind of killer we were looking for. The body of the mother provided the proof.'

Dupin opened the book at the page marked by the envelope. Then he opened the envelope and took from it ten or twelve red-brown hairs.

'The fingers of Madame Espanaye's right hand were shut tight,' he said, 'and I wondered why. When I opened them, I found these hairs in her hand.'

I looked at the hairs closely. They were thick and rough, rather like the hairs of a brush. 'They are not – not from a man's head, Dupin.'

'No. And the marks on the daughter's neck were not made by a man's hands either. I made this drawing of the marks I found.' He showed me a drawing on the front of the envelope.

'Then, who – what – ?' I imagined the old lady struggling with the killer. She had pulled out some red-brown hairs . . . she was still holding them when she died. It was a terrible thought.

Dupin pointed to the middle of a page in the book. 'Read this,' he said. 'It's about wild animals in the forests of Borneo.'

I read: 'One of the biggest members of the monkey family is a creature called the orang-utan. It is very strong, very active and very fierce. Although it spends a lot of its time in the trees of the forest, it may attack people and kill them. The orang-utan's thick hair is red-brown in colour . . . '

The next part described the appearance of the animal, its size, its 'arms', legs, 'fingers' and 'voice'. There were two or three pictures.

'You see,' said Dupin, 'the creature's fingers fit the marks in my drawing. The hair is the same, too. And an orang-utan could easily spring from the rain-water pipe to the window.'

I understood at once the truth about the terrible murders. 'So it was an orang-utan that killed the women!' I cried. 'Who would have thought of that? But, Dupin – one of the voices was a man's voice. Didn't he say something in French?'

'I cannot explain that, but we will soon know. A man – probably the owner of the beast – might have seen the murders. The two voices were shouting angrily. No doubt the man was angry because the animal had killed the women. The creature might have escaped from him. Perhaps he had followed it to the house and tried to catch it. We do not know exactly what happened.'

'Then – the animal may still be free,' I said.

'I hope so! If it is, and if the man is not guilty of murder, he will come to this house today. On our way home yesterday, I stopped at a newspaper office. I asked for a notice to be put in this morning's paper. It is the paper that gives a lot of news about ships, and so sailors read it.'

Dupin gave me a newspaper, and I read:

> *Caught* – In the City Gardens, two days ago, a large red-brown orang-utan of the Borneo kind. The owner, who is a sailor, can have the animal back if he pays a few necessary charges. Call at Number 7, Rue Genève.

I said, 'A sailor? How do you know that?'

'I think it is correct,' Dupin replied, taking from his pocket a piece of red silk ribbon. 'I found this ribbon at the bottom of the pipe outside Madame Espanaye's house. As you see, it is rather dirty, and it has the smell of hair-oil on it. Sailors often tie up their hair with a ribbon like this.'

'But – won't the man be afraid to come here?'

'If he is not guilty, why should he be afraid? He may say to himself, "I did not kill those women. I am a poor man, but I can sell my orang-utan for a lot of money. Why should I lose the animal? It was found in the City Gardens – a long way from Rue Morgue. The police are puzzled about the murders: how can anyone know that my orang-utan killed the women?" '

'Yes, I see. The police might never guess that it was an animal.'

'The man may wonder how we know that he owns the beast. But he is a sailor – a brave man, and probably honest. Very few sailors are dishonest. These events must be troubling him, of course, and he will not really want to hide from trouble. He may even be very glad after I – '

Just at that moment the door-bell rang.

'Keep your hand on your pistol,' Dupin said quietly. 'But do not take it out unless we have trouble.' Then he called loudly – 'Come in, please!'

A man opened the door and walked in. He certainly looked like a sailor: he was tall and strong, with a happy, honest, brown face, and a thick beard. He had a stick in his hand, but carried no other arms. His black hair was tied up behind his head with a ribbon. He bowed to us and said, 'Good evening.'

'Sit down, please,' said Dupin. 'You have come about the orang-utan, I think. He is a very fine animal, and a valuable one, too. How old is he?'

The sailor took a long, deep breath and sat down. He looked suddenly glad. 'I don't know exactly,' he said. 'He may be four or five years old. Have you got him here?'

'Oh, no. We have no place for him here. A friend of mine who used to keep horses is taking care of him. But you can have him in the morning. Can you describe him – just to prove that you are the owner?'

'Yes, sir, I can describe him. And I will give you something for your trouble, but – but I am not a rich man.'

'Well – thank you,' Dupin said. 'I have not spent very much on the animal, and so – what shall I ask for? Let me think.'

My friend got up and walked slowly to the door. He locked the door and put the key in his pocket. Then he took out his pistol, laying it calmly on the table.

He looked at the visitor and said, 'I do not want any money. But there is something else: tell me everything you know about the murders in Rue Morgue.'

The sailor's face turned grey. He stood up, breathing quickly and holding his stick tightly. The next moment, he fell back on to his chair. His whole body was shaking.

'You need not be afraid,' Dupin said in a kind voice.

'We may be able to help you. We shall certainly not harm you – I promise that. I know that you did not kill those two women. I am also sure that you know some of the facts. Let me explain.

'You could do nothing to help the women – although you tried. There was a lot of money in the house, but you did not take it. So no one can blame you. You know that the police have taken Adolphe Lebon to prison. They think that he killed the women. But he is not guilty – you know that, too. You are a man of honour, I think; and so you will agree with me. Lebon must be set free today.'

For a moment the sailor did not reply. There was still a look of fear on his face. Then he rested his stick against the arm of the chair.

'All right,' he said. 'I will try to tell you. You already know some of the facts – or I would not be here. I hope that you will believe this – this terrible story. I am not guilty. I swear it! I will tell you . . . '

This is the story that he told us.

He had caught the orang-utan in the East, and had brought it back to France, hoping to sell it. In Paris he had rented a house and locked the beast in a spare room.

On the day of the murders, he had come home at two o'clock in the morning. The orang-utan had broken out of its room and was cutting up food with the sailor's knife. The knife was long and very sharp – a dangerous thing for such a wild beast to play with.

The sailor picked up the stick, with which he had been trying to train the creature. Seeing the stick, the orang-utan ran out of the room, jumped through an open window and reached the street. It still had the knife.

The sailor followed. It was then nearly three o'clock, and the streets were quiet. The animal turned into a dark street behind Rue Morgue. It saw the light shining from the open window at the top of Madame Espanaye's house. At the same time, it noticed the rain-water pipe at the corner. With great speed it climbed up the pipe and sprang across the space to the window, straight into the room. The whole exercise, from the street to the room, took less than a minute.

The sailor was very anxious, though in one way he was glad. The orang-utan would soon have to come back down that pipe; and then he would be able to catch it. But he was afraid of the trouble the animal might cause inside. After a moment or two, he decided to follow it.

Being a sailor, he climbed the pipe easily enough. But when he reached the height of the window, he could not go any further. If he had tried to spring across the space, he would have fallen. So he leaned outwards from the pipe, and could then see inside the room. The sight that met the sailor's eyes almost made him fall from the pipe.

The orang-utan seized Madame Espanaye's hair. She fought with the creature and made it angry. With one great swing of the knife, her head was almost cut off. The sight of blood then made the beast really mad. It turned upon the daughter, caught her fiercely by the neck and swung her around in the air until her neck broke.

The orang-utan suddenly saw its master's face outside the window, and its madness changed at once to fear. It rushed around the room, looking for a place to hide the bodies. It was then that the furniture and other things were broken and thrown about.

The creature seized the daughter's body and pushed it up the chimney. Then it picked up the body of Madame Espanaye and threw it out of the open window. The sailor, very frightened, had been trying to calm the beast. His voice, and the orang-utan's fierce sounds, were heard by the people on the stairs.

Shaking with fear, the sailor slid down the pipe to the ground. He had decided to hurry home, hoping that he would never see his orang-utan again. But he looked back once.

The animal had climbed out of the window. With one great blow of its powerful arm, it struck at the window and shut it. Then it sprang on to the pipe. The sailor raced away.

There is not much more to say. Two days later, the sailor himself caught the orang-utan, and sold it to the Director of the Animal Gardens of Paris. But before that, Dupin, the sailor and I had talked to Georges Godinot, the head of the police.

Georges was friendly enough to Dupin, but he was rather ashamed, too. It was unfair, he thought, that someone *outside* the police had found the answer to the mystery. Lebon was set free at once. As we left Georges's office, we heard someone say: 'Other people should not try to do the work of the police.'

Dupin did not trouble to reply.

5

DOWN INTO THE MAELSTROM

One summer, I went to the north of Norway, and stayed on one of the islands called Lofoten. It was there that I met the man in this story. He offered to guide me to the top of the highest rock on the island.

We set out one morning, and reached the place about midday. For several minutes then, the old man was too breathless to talk. I stood looking straight down a wall of rock to the sea, five hundred metres below.

Then the old man said, 'Not long ago I could climb up here like a boy. I can't do it now. You think that I am old. I am not. I am only thirty-six. But my body and my spirit are like those of an old man.'

I was very surprised to hear that, because he did look old. I had thought that he was about sixty-five.

'Three years ago, something terrible happened to me down there,' he went on, pointing to the wild, dark sea below. 'I do not think that a man has ever had a worse experience – and lived after it. It lasted for six hours. In that time, my hair changed colour from black to white. My strength and courage left me for ever. I am afraid now to look over this cliff, as you are looking.

'From these rocks you can see the place where it happened. But let us go a little lower. It will be quieter there when the Maelstrom begins! And I shall not be so afraid.'

We moved a few steps down and sat looking out to sea. We could see two islands: the larger one was about five kilometres away; the small one was two kilometres nearer the shore. The sea between us and the further island looked very unusual. Thousands of little waves flowed this way and that way, in every direction.

My companion said, 'The bigger island is Vurrgh. The other one is called Moskoe. Can you hear anything now? Can you see anything strange in the water?'

There was a growing sound – as if a hundred running horses were coming nearer. The waves flowed faster and faster, but now in one direction only – towards the east.

In a few minutes, as I was watching, the water seemed to boil. The roughest part was between the little island of Moskoe and the coast. There, the waves rose and rushed along, turning in a thousand racing circles – but always towards the east.

The picture changed quickly. The sea moved faster, but its surface grew flat. The little racing whirlpools spread out far, and began to form one huge circle. All at once, this great circle of rushing water, more than two kilometres wide, could be clearly seen.

The edge of the giant whirlpool was a wide band of white water, circling madly. The inside of the circle was a flat, shining, sloping wall of black water. I could not see the bottom of it. Round and round the whirlpool flew, with a terrible noise.

The rock where we were sitting shook with the force of it. I was so frightened that I lay down on my face, holding the rock tightly.

'Is this,' I cried to my friend ' – is this the great Maelstrom?'

'Yes, but here we call it the Moskoe-strom.'

I had read about it in two or three books. But I had never imagined that it could be so fearful.

'What causes the whirlpool?' I asked.

My friend replied, 'It depends on the tide. There is a short time, just at high tide and just at low tide, when the sea is calm.'

'And how long does the whirlpool last?'

'From beginning to end, six hours – while the tide is rising; and six hours again while it is going down. Between the two, the sea is calm for about fifteen minutes.'

'Is it always as noisy as this?'

A great circle of rushing water.

'In winter it is worse! Hundreds of ships, big and small, have been lost in it. If they sail too near it, they are drawn into the whirlpool and pulled to the bottom of the sea. There, they are broken to pieces against the rocks. Nothing can help them, nothing can save them. When the tide turns, the broken pieces are thrown up to the surface.'

After a time, my companion touched my arm, and said, 'Well, you have seen it now. Let us go behind this rock, away from the noise. I will tell you what happened to me. I am the only man alive who has been down into the Moskoe-strom.'

We moved to the back of the rock, and he began to talk.

'I and my two brothers had a small ship, and we used to fish around these islands. There were plenty of fish – because we three were the only men brave enough to fish here! We always had to sail past the Moskoe-strom in the short time when it was quiet.

'My brothers and I knew exactly when the tide would turn: so we could sail safely past. We always made sure of the wind, too, before we left home. This went on for six or seven years, and we made only two mistakes about the weather. Both times, we were able to wait in a safe place until the storm ended.

'We always crossed the Moskoe-strom without accident, but we had to be careful. Fifteen minutes is not long to sail a ship past that dangerous place. Sometimes we were a minute or two early or late, and then we felt afraid. For it *is* a terrible danger, as you saw for yourself.

'Well, three years ago, on July 18th, we decided to go fishing, as usual. All the morning, there was a gentle wind from the south-west, and no clouds in the sky. We sailed past the strom at about two o'clock – in the calm between the afternoon tides.

'We caught a lot of fish that day – more, I think, than we had ever caught before. At seven o'clock in the evening, we left the fishing grounds. The evening calm would be at eight o'clock; and so we had an hour to reach the strom and sail past it safely.

'We had been going well for some time when, quite suddenly, the wind changed. Strange, brown clouds moved up fast behind us. It grew so dark that we could not see each other in the ship. Almost at once a storm began.

'It was the worst storm that I could remember. When it began, my younger brother was blown straight into the sea, and lost. I would have been blown off, too, but I was lying flat in the middle of the boat, holding an iron ring.

'Huge waves rushed over the ship, and carried away everything that was not fixed. For half a minute, the water covered me. Then, still holding the ring, I struggled to raise my head. I took a few deep breaths. A hand touched my arm. It was my elder brother, still alive. I felt very glad that he was safe.

' "*Moskoe-strom*!" he shouted into my ear.

'My gladness changed at once to fear. The word made me shake like a sick man. I knew its meaning. I knew exactly what he wanted me to understand. The storm was driving us fast towards the whirlpool, and we might reach it before the calm.

'But there was nothing that we could do. All our sails had been blown away. The ship was racing through seas like mountains. Although it was still very dark, the sky had changed a little. Looking up for a moment, I saw a circle of clear sky – with the full moon shining in it.

'It lit up the wild ocean clearly. I looked at my watch. I knew that it must have stopped when the water had covered me. But I was wrong. It had stopped at *seven o'clock* – before the storm had begun. We were late. The tide had already turned. The whirlpool was already in full force!

'A great wave carried the ship high up on the water. I looked around quickly in the light of the moon. One look was enough. I knew exactly where we were. The Moskoe-strom was four hundred metres in front of us. I could hear the noise of it above the wind. I closed my eyes. I felt more afraid than I had ever felt in my life.

'We travelled those four hundred metres in less than three minutes. Then we entered the wide band of white water that surrounded the whirlpool. The ship turned inwards a little – and immediately raced away, around the strom. We were in the great circle of the whirlpool.

'The wind dropped. The sound had grown to a frightening howl. I thought that our ship would quickly fall to the bottom of the whirlpool. The sea rose on our left side like a great, turning wall of water. On our right, we could not see the bottom of the pool. Our speed around the huge circle was increasing every minute.

'It was quite certain then that our ship could never escape. Soon – I did not know how long – she would be broken to pieces on the rocks at the bottom. My brother and I would die. Those thoughts were clear in my mind, and, in a strange way, they took away my fear.

'We travelled fast around the edge of the pool for about an hour, slowly drawing nearer and nearer to the terrible, *sloping*, inner surface. I still had the iron ring in my hands. My brother was holding a small, empty water-barrel that was tied down by a rope.

'He suddenly left his barrel and rushed to me. With the fear and the strength of a madman, he pulled my hands from the ring and took it himself. I felt very sorry when that happened. But it did not matter at all. Soon, we would both be dead. So I let him have the ring, and I went to the barrel.

'Just as I reached it, our ship turned wildly inwards, and shot down into the pool. I shut my eyes and said a quick prayer. I thought it was the end. I expected sudden death. But it did not come.

'A moment later, the ship stopped falling. I waited a minute. I was still alive. I opened my eyes. I will never forget the sight around me.

'The ship was hanging half way down the side of the whirlpool. The pool, shaped like a huge V, was four hundred metres deep and a thousand metres across. The water, turning madly, looked like a wall of black oil. Everything was lit up by the bright light of the moon.

'For two or three minutes, I just looked at this terrible, this wonderful, sight. But it was five minutes before I could think clearly. Then I noticed a strange thing. The side of the whirlpool sloped downwards steeply, but our ship was travelling around in her usual way. I mean – she was sailing well, and no water came into her. Although we were moving very fast, it was easy for us to stand up.

'As I said, the ship had immediately fallen about half way down the whirlpool. But after that first fall, our movement towards the bottom was slow. We raced round and round, each circle taking us only about a metre lower. There was plenty of time, then, for me to look around.

'I soon saw that our ship was not the only thing in the pool. Above us and below us, all round the pool, there were many other things: broken parts of other ships and boats, dead trees, boxes and sticks, and even a few barrels. I looked at all these things, especially the ones that were near us. Having nothing else to do, I tried to guess which thing would next disappear at the bottom of the pool.

'Once I said to myself, "That tree will surely be the next." I was wrong. An old boat, bigger than ours, passed the tree on its way down. The boat made five more circles of the pool, and then dropped suddenly out of sight.

'My guesses were usually wrong, and after a time I wondered why. An exciting idea came into my head, and I watched the pool carefully. Two minutes later, my legs began to shake. It was not fear that made them shake. It was hope!

'I understood suddenly that a big object travelled faster down the whirlpool than a small one. Some small things – pieces of wood and boxes – might never reach the bottom. The tide would turn, and end the whirlpool, while they were still going around in circles. And what would happen to them then? I guessed that they would be thrown up to the surface of the sea.

'I watched a yellow barrel that was circling the pool. It had been quite near us before, but now it was high above. Our ship was going down a lot faster than that barrel.

'I did not waste another minute. I untied my water-barrel from the ship. I made signs to my brother, and pointed to other small things in the water. I do not know whether he understood or not. He just shook his head at me and refused to leave the ring.

'There seemed no time to lose. I quickly tied myself to

the barrel. There was enough rope for my brother, too, and I showed it to him. But he shook his head again. So I would have to leave him to his fate. The next moment, I threw myself and the barrel into the water.

'The result was exactly as I had hoped. I am alive now, as you see. I did escape from the Moskoe-strom – in the way that I have explained.

'For a long time, our ship and my barrel continued to travel around the whirlpool. The ship went down fifty metres below me. I saw it turn wildly then – three times in less than a minute. And at once it fell into the angry water round the rocks at the bottom of the pool. I never saw my brother again.

'My barrel circled for another hour or more, slowly going lower and lower. But it was still a long way from the bottom when the whirlpool began to change. The slope of the side grew less steep. My speed dropped. The bottom of the pool seemed to rise towards me. The tide was turning.

'The sky was clear. The full moon was lower in the west. My barrel and I rose up slowly to the surface. There was still a strong wind, and the sea was rough. The wind blew me far down the coast, to the usual fishing grounds. Some fishermen in a ship saw me and pulled me out of the water.

'Those men were from our own village. They were my friends – but they did not know me. My hair had been black the day before. It was as white then as you see it now. I could not talk to them for more than an hour. When at last I did tell them my story, they refused to believe it.

'I have now told it to you – and I can hardly expect you to believe it.'

6

THE PIT AND THE PENDULUM

This story describes events that may have happened a hundred and fifty, or more, years ago. In those days, men were punished if their religious beliefs did not agree with the beliefs of the church. The judges were leaders of the church.

Such religious courts came to an end in 1834.

For many hours I had stood, with my arms tied to my sides. Then my trial came to an end, and the judges were ready to order punishment. The ropes were untied, and I was allowed to sit down.

There were bright lights in front of my eyes. I saw the black clothes of the judges. I heard them say that I must die, and then the voices faded. I could not hear or feel anything. The judges' white lips were still moving. They were explaining *how* I must die. I could hear nothing, and my body began to shake.

A wonderful thought came to my mind. It was like the sound of music: the thought of the sweet rest that I should find in the grave. Tall men carried me along dark passages and down steep stairs. Down, down, down . . . They laid me on a floor. The floor was flat and cold and wet. I felt tired and afraid.

A long time later, I felt something moving, and there were sounds in my ears. The movement and the sounds came from my own beating heart! I began to think then – and remembered the trial and the judges. I moved my hands and feet. There were no ropes around me. I did not open my eyes.

I was lying on my back. I wanted to open my eyes, but was afraid of seeing – only *darkness*. I struggled with my fear, and after a time opened my eyes quickly. Darkness! Complete blackness! I fought for breath. The blackness was like a weight on me. Where was I?

A terrible fear suddenly made me shake. Was I already in my grave – *alive*? I stood up and stretched my arms above my head. I turned slowly, with my arms stretched out. I touched nothing. I walked forward a little. There was still nothing. I felt better. A grave would not be as large as this room was.

I went on slowly until my hands touched a wall. Like the floor, it was flat, cold and wet. I decided then to try to measure the room if I could. I was wearing a long prison shirt. Tearing a strip of cloth from the bottom of it, I put one end of the strip against the wall and stretched the rest on the floor. My idea was to walk around the walls, counting my steps, until I returned to the cloth.

But I had only gone eight steps when I slipped on the wet floor. I fell forward and just lay there, too tired to get up.

I must have slept for a time. When I woke, and stretched out my hand, I felt a loaf of bread and a jar of water beside me. I ate and drank gladly, and afterwards went on around the walls.

I had counted fifty steps when my foot touched the cloth again; and so the room was about thirty metres around. I then wanted to know the shape of the room, and began to walk slowly across the floor.

After ten steps, I slipped and fell again, but this time I almost fainted with fear. My body was lying flat on the floor, face downwards. Under my head there was –

nothing!

A strange smell, like dead leaves, rose up around me. I stretched out my arm. I had fallen at the edge of a pit! I broke off a piece of stone and dropped it into the hole. It struck the side as it fell, and then, after a few seconds, it struck water. There was a noise from the roof, and a quick, sudden light shone down on me. Then darkness again.

I now knew part of the fate that the judges had prepared for me! If I had not slipped and fallen, I would have walked straight into the pit. I would have died there – very slowly. And who would ever know about it? The court liked that kind of secret, sudden end. Well, I had escaped from slow death in the pit; but what else had been prepared for me?

I drew back, frightened, to the wall. Were there other pits in the room? I stayed awake for a long time, thinking of danger. At last, I lay down on the floor and slept.

When I woke up, I found more bread and another jar of water beside me. The water had a strange taste, but I was thirsty and drank it at once. There was probably something in it, to make me sleep; because I just could not stay awake. I must have slept for several hours.

The room was not dark when I opened my eyes the next time. A bright light was shining into it, but I could not see where the light came from. The room was square. Its walls did not look like stone walls. They seemed to be large, flat, metal plates, and they were covered with terrible paintings of devils. The colours of these pictures had faded, but the drawings were still clear. The floor of the room was made of stone, and the round pit was in the middle of it. There were no other pits.

I saw all this in a few seconds, although I could hardly

move. I was lying on my back on a low bed. I could move my head and one arm, but the rest of my body was tied tightly to the bed by a long rope. I could just reach a plate of meat on the floor beside me. I was thirstier than ever, but the water had gone.

The room was ten or twelve metres high. The roof also seemed to be metal, painted over with terrible figures. The picture directly above my bed was, I believe, the figure of Old Father Time, with an instrument in his hands. At least, I thought that the figure was holding an instrument like the pendulum of a clock.

But a moment later, I noticed that the pendulum was moving slightly. It was swinging just a little, backwards and forwards. So that short bar, with something on its end, was not a fixed part of the picture. I watched it for a few minutes, until a noise from the pit made me look in that direction.

Several big rats climbed out of the pit and crossed the floor towards me. Others followed – many others. They were all hurrying hungrily towards my plate of meat. I was kept very busy, beating them away with my hand.

It was an hour, or more perhaps, before I looked up again to the roof. The movement of the pendulum was now greater than before, and faster too. It was swinging about a metre each way, forwards and backwards. But I was frightened by two other things that I noticed. The pendulum was *nearer* to me than before; and its lower end was – a long, sharp knife! The shining steel edge curved upwards at the ends, and made a soft sound as it moved through the air.

How can I describe my feelings? I lay for many hours, watching and counting the swings of that terrible

Several big rats climbed out of the pit.

knife. The downward movement, towards me, was very, very slow. But little by little, it *was* coming nearer; though, even at the end of that first day, the knife was only a metre from the roof.

All through the night, I heard the soft cry of the steel through the air. All through the night, I had to drive away the rats. In the morning, the knife was another metre nearer.

Days passed – several days and nights. I was very tired and almost mad with fear. The rats would not let me sleep. Now the knife was swinging so closely over me that I could feel the wind of its passing. The smell of the cold steel was strong in my nose. I lay there, smiling at death, as a child smiles at a jewel.

I slept, or perhaps I fainted. I do not know. When I opened my eyes again, the rats had eaten most of my meat. I drove them away and took the last pieces for myself. As I put some into my mouth, the germ of an idea – the light of a hope! – grew in my mind. I struggled to make it complete.

The pendulum was moving across my body – above my heart. The knife would first touch the cloth of my shirt. On the next swing, it would cut a little deeper; then deeper again. Each swing was now several metres long – half way across the room and back again. Although the knife was moving fast through the air, it would not cut into my body for several minutes yet. I watched it as it flew over me.

It swung towards me – down – away from me – down. Far to the right – down – far to the left – down; with the terrible *whisper* of death.

I struggled against the rope that held me. I turned my head from side to side. I opened and shut my eyes as the bright steel flew over me. I wished that I could die quickly!

Suddenly I felt calm. My thoughts were wonderfully clear. The rope that tied me down was in one piece. It did not cross my chest; and so the knife would never cut the rope. But if *something* cut it, I could quickly free myself. By then, the knife would be very close!

The hope in my breast grew suddenly strong. The rats! The rats could help me!

For days they had surrounded my bed, waiting for me to die. They had climbed over me and bitten my hand when I drove them away. They were mad with hunger. If I did not move on the bed, they always tried to reach my face.

I looked at the plate. There were still three pieces of meat, soft pieces with a bad smell. I picked them up, and rubbed them hard on the rope in three or four different places. Then I rested my left arm on the bed and lay without moving.

The leader of the rats immediately sprang on to the bed and began to smell the rope. The others followed, and more came out of the pit. They climbed over me. In a few moments, fifty or sixty rats were on top of me. I shut my eyes.

The swing of the pendulum did not trouble them at all. They were accustomed to it, and so kept easily out of its way! They tore at the rope where I had rubbed the meat. They were a heavy weight on my body. I could hardly breathe. I felt them around my neck. Their cold lips pressed against mine. I did not move.

'A minute more,' I thought. 'Can I bear this for one minute more?'

The rope was moving! It was pulled in two – three –

places! I heard it break! And again it broke! I did not move. The knife cut through my shirt. I could not wait another second.

I waved my arm. The rats ran off – taking most of the rope. The knife swung down. A sharp pain crossed my chest. I slid sideways off the bed, on to the floor. I was free! I had escaped from the pendulum.

I was free – but still in prison. As soon as I had left the bed, the terrible pendulum stopped swinging. It was pulled up quite suddenly to the roof. Someone, up there, was watching me. Someone had seen me slide off the bed. And I had no doubt that some other devilish punishment was ready for me.

There *was* something different about the metal walls of the room, but I did not know what it was. The light in the room was brighter than before. When I looked anxiously around, I saw where the light was coming from.

It came from a narrow space between the walls and the floor. This space ran all round the room, and so the walls were separate from the floor. There was the same kind of space between the walls and the roof.

The terrible paintings around me were bright with fire! When I had first seen them, their colours were faded. But now they seemed alive with light and colour. The eyes shone at me with real fire! The room had grown very hot – filled with the smell of hot iron. I fought for breath.

I thought of the pit and moved to the edge of it. It would be cool down there, I thought, as I looked into it. The light from the burning roof shone down to the bottom. But I could hardly believe the thing that I saw there! Oh, those cruel judges! I could bear any kind of death – but not death in the pit! I turned away, crying, and covered my face with my hands.

The room was even hotter. I opened my eyes. The walls were red with heat – and moving! Two opposite corners were drawing nearer to the pit. The other two were moving further apart. I was in a burning box that was slowly being pressed flat!

I ran to one of the further corners and burned myself. 'Any death,' I cried, 'but not the pit!' I guessed then that the walls were coming together on purpose – to force me into the pit! I struggled to keep away from it. Could I bear the red heat of those walls for long?

At last, I knew that I could not. The walls forced me to the edge. There was hardly room for my feet on the floor. All hope left me. I stopped my struggles. I looked up and gave one long, loud cry. One foot was pushed over the edge. I closed my eyes.

Suddenly I heard voices. There were loud cries – and shots. The burning walls moved back! A man's strong arm took mine and pulled me – just as I was falling into the pit.

The French army had entered the town.

I was saved.

Mr and Mrs Moissart

|

their daughter, Miss Moissart, *married* Victor Voissart

|

their daughter, Miss Voissart, *married* Mr Croissart

|

their daughter, Marie Croissart, *married* Charles Froissart

|

Napoleon Froissart (their son)
(also called Napoleon Simpson)

7

THE SPECTACLES

First, I must tell you about myself. I am still a young man, not yet twenty-two years old. My name, at present, is Simpson, and that is a common name in America. But it has been my name only for a year – in fact, since the death of an old gentleman called Adolphus Simpson.

I never met Mr Adolphus Simpson in my life, but he was a distant relation of my family. When he died, last year, he left a hundred thousand dollars to me – on condition that I changed my name to Simpson. Not many people are willing to change their family names, and I was not very eager to change mine. It was Froissart, and I was proud of it – because of its important place in French history. But a hundred thousand dollars is a lot of money, and so I changed my name by law. And for the past year, I have been called Napoleon Simpson.

Before going on, I want to tell you another thing about the names in my family. My father was Charles Froissart, of Paris. My mother, before her marriage, was called

Marie Croissart. Her mother was the eldest daughter of Victor Voissart; and Mr Voissart's wife, before her marriage, was named Moissart. So here we have Moissart, Voissart, Croissart and Froissart – all in a direct line. You will agree that that is a very curious thing. It is interesting, but unimportant, that the three ladies got married before their sixteenth birthdays.

I am a tall, strong and good-looking young man. My hair is black and wavy. My nose is straight. My eyes are large and grey. Though my eye-sight is very weak indeed, no one would guess that by looking at me. Still, the weakness is unfortunate and sometimes troubles me. Of course, a dozen doctors have advised me to wear glasses. I do not like glasses, because they *never* improve a young man's looks. They make him look anxious, or frightened, or older than his years, and so I have always refused to wear them. Luckily, I have never needed to work, and so my weak sight is not a very serious problem.

You know, now, what I am like. I will only add that I have an active and an eager mind. I like to decide things quickly – and carry them out at once. All my life I have loved and respected women.

One night last winter, I went to a theatre in New York, with my friend Mr Talbot. The show was a very good one, and the theatre was full. Talbot likes music very much, and so his eyes hardly left the singers and dancers. I was quite happy to look around at all the famous and wealthy people who were there.

I had been doing that for half an hour, perhaps, when I suddenly noticed a fresh and delightful face. The lady was sitting with her friends in one of the boxes at the side of the theatre.

If I live for a thousand years, I will never forget my excitement. I said to myself, 'There is a goddess among women!' The face, the whole shape of the head and shoulders, was the most beautiful I had ever seen. To me, the form of a lovely woman is like magic. And this woman possessed beauty that I had never imagined.

I looked at her for at least half an hour, as if I had been made of stone. During all that time, I felt the full force and the truth of love. Before, I had always laughed at the words 'love at first sight'. It had seemed impossible for any man to *love* a woman as soon as he saw her. But now I knew that it *was* possible. Indeed, love at first sight must be the only true love. A powerful and mysterious force was drawing me to this lady. I saw – I felt – I knew that I was deeply in love with her.

While I was watching her, a few noisy people got up to leave the theatre. Everyone turned to look at them. The lady also turned, giving me a different view of her face. She was even more beautiful than I had thought. But something disappointed me, too, though I could not quite explain it. Perhaps 'disappointed' is not the right word. I felt less excited but not less happy. There was strength and a sort of comfort in the lady's face. There was something else as well. Was it – experience, I wondered? It troubled me a little, but interested me very much.

I had already decided to meet her. I wanted to meet her at once! If she had been alone, I would have forgotten all my manners. I would have gone to her box! Fortunately, a gentleman was with her, and another very beautiful woman who seemed a few years younger than my goddess. But if I could not talk to her, I had to talk to somebody about her.

A mysterious force was drawing me to this lady.

'Talbot,' I said, 'listen to me. Do you see that box? – there ! – no, not that one, the next one. Have you ever seen such a lovely woman?'

Talbot looked carelessly at the box – 'Yes, she is very beautiful – ' and then turned again to the dancers.

'Who is she?' I asked.

'She is Madame Lalande, now the most beautiful woman in New York. Very wealthy, too, and a widow. She has just arrived from Paris.'

'Do you know her?'

'Of course.'

'Can I meet her? It is love, Talbot – at first sight!'

'Certainly. When shall I arrange it? – And where?'

'Tomorrow, at your house. At one o'clock.'

'All right. Now please be quiet. I want to listen to the music.'

I asked him more questions, but he just refused to answer. So, for a long time, I kept my eyes fixed on Madame Lalande. She was a picture of loveliness, but there was still something that I did not understand. Was it her seriousness? Her sadness? Her tenderness? Had the long voyage from France made her tired? I did not know what it was. But I loved it with all my heart.

Then, suddenly, I felt weak. Madame Lalande had noticed me! She was looking at me! I could not turn away. Her eyes held mine, like magic. She herself turned away, but only for a minute. Then she looked at me again – to see if I was still looking at her! Her beautiful eyes fell at once. A delightful colour appeared in her face. She did not turn away.

Instead, she raised a small pair of theatre-glasses to her eyes. Through them, she studied me carefully for four or five minutes.

I was very surprised. I would have been angry if any

other woman had done that. But Madame Lalande was – well, she was the love of my heart! She examined me so calmly and so naturally that I felt only surprise.

After those five minutes, her eyes moved again to the dancers. At least, I thought so. But I soon realised my mistake. She was only pretending to watch the show! From the corner of her eye, she was still looking at me! You can imagine how I felt.

Ten minutes later, she spoke to the gentleman with her. They both looked straight at me, and then he answered her. I knew that they were talking about me. Later, and for a long time, she studied me through her glasses.

Her simple, unashamed manner only made me love her more. I felt brave – even wild! I was ready for any madness! I waited for my chance. After a time it came. All eyes – except hers and mine – were on the show. I bowed slightly to her.

Her face grew red. She looked around slowly to see if others had noticed me bowing. Then she leaned towards the gentleman beside her.

She was telling him, I thought. I had been very stupid. . . . . But nothing happened. Madame Lalande just gave the gentleman a programme! The next moment, she let her eyes meet mine quite firmly. A faint smile showed the bright line of her pearly teeth. She bent her head once – twice! – towards me. That could have only one meaning. It meant 'Yes'.

My heart seemed to have the wings of a bird. I need not tell you my feelings – the thousand feelings that rose at once in my breast. I was as happy as any man could be. I was in love. It was my *first* real love. It was love at first sight; and at first sight, too, she had returned it. I could not doubt that Madame Lalande loved me. She loved me as blindly as I loved her.

The show ended, and everyone got up to leave the theatre. I struggled to reach the lady's side, but the crowd was too great. I could not get near her. 'Tomorrow will soon come,' I said to myself. 'Tomorrow I shall meet her at Talbot's house.'

After a sleepless night, I did not get up early. At exactly one o'clock I knocked at Talbot's door and asked for my friend.

'He's out, sir,' the servant said.

'Out!' I cried. 'That isn't true! What do you mean?'

'Mr Talbot is out, sir. He isn't at home. He left early this morning, for a week's holiday in the country.'

I was so angry that I wanted to hit the man. I could not say anything at all. I turned round, silently cursing the whole family of Talbots. My useless friend was not a man of honour. He had forgotten our appointment as soon as we had made it!

I walked slowly and miserably along the street. Several other friends were passing. I asked them all if they knew Madame Lalande. Everyone had heard of her, and a few knew her face. But no one had met her. I was talking to three fellows at a busy corner when a carriage rolled towards us.

'There – there she is!' the first man cried.

'And very beautiful!' the second said.

'A jewel from heaven!' the third agreed.

I looked. It was an open carriage, moving slowly. Madame Lalande was sitting in it, with the younger lady who had been with her at the theatre.

'Her companion still looks lovely, too,' the first fellow

said.

Someone said, 'She looks better than she did in Paris five years ago. The French know how to preserve a face and figure. Don't you think so, Froissart? – Simpson, I mean.'

'Beside Madame Lalande,' I said, 'well – she is like a candle beside the evening star.'

'Ah, yes, you *are* clever, Simpson.'

My friends left me then, and I went on, feeling very excited. Madame Lalande had seen me! She had seen me – and smiled! How could I meet her? That was my big problem. There seemed to be nothing that I could do, except wait for Talbot.

Every day I went to his house. He had not returned. Every day I visited one of the best places of amusement, hoping to see the lady. Two weeks passed: Talbot was still away. I began to feel quite hopeless. Madame Lalande had come from Paris. She would probably go back there before Talbot came home. I would never see her again! That thought was too terrible to bear. I was almost in a state of madness.

Then, one evening, I saw her again at the theatre. Many wonderful looks and smiles passed between us. Just before the end of the show, I decided to do something. Getting up from my seat, I left the theatre and waited outside.

I followed Madame Lalande's carriage to her house, and so found her address. That night, I wrote her a long letter, telling her of my love.

'I want you to know,' I wrote, 'that I shall always love you as much as I do now. I am quite sure that you love me. If you leave New York before we can meet, I shall certainly die . . . '

I did not hide anything from her. I told her that I was wealthy and in good health. I even explained the weakness of my eyes. And I ended the letter with an offer of marriage.

I waited fearfully for her reply. Four days later – it seemed a hundred years! – the reply came. Yes, the beautiful Madame Lalande wrote to me, and she repeated the message of her beautiful eyes. She was a true French-woman!

She did not care about customs, she wrote. She obeyed only her own heart. She did not refuse my love – and did not hide her feelings behind a veil of silence. Her letter ended:

'Mr Simpson will forgive me. I do not write often in English, but I am learning quickly! I will only say this – Mr Simpson has guessed the truth! Need I say more? Haven't I already said too much?

Eugenie Lalande.'

I kissed the letter a thousand times. But Talbot still did not return. I wrote to him and explained my suffering. He wrote back: important business was delaying him. He begged me to keep calm. 'Read some history books,' he said, 'and you will feel better.'

'He is a fool,' I thought. 'If he can't come himself, why doesn't he write to Madame Lalande?' I wrote to him again, and begged him to do that. If he sent the letter to me, I could deliver it to her.

Talbot's servant sent my letter back, with a note: 'Mr Talbot has gone to Canada. I do not know his address; and I do not know when he is coming back.'

I cursed Talbot, his family and his servant. But curses did not help me. I would have to arrange something myself. Madame Lalande had smiled at me, and I had smiled at her. We had written love letters to each other. Did I have to wait for Talbot? Would it be terrible if – if I just met her in the street and spoke to her?

Since our letters, I had walked past her house twenty times a day. I had seen the carriage leaving and returning. In the evenings, just before dark, I knew that Madame Lalande often went for a walk. Only a servant – an old man – went with her. They used to walk round a public garden in front of her house. One evening I waited for her among the trees and flowers. It was almost dark.

I had to deceive the old man. And so I spoke to her as if we had been friends for a long time. She understood at once. She greeted me in the same way, holding out a little hand for me to kiss. The servant moved away. And so, with full hearts, we talked of our love. I asked her to marry me. 'Soon, madam,' I said. 'Next week, if you agree.'

She smiled at my eagerness – and begged me to wait. 'Your friends, Mr Simpson – they know that we haven't really met. Only a few days ago, someone told me that you wished to meet me. I do not care about your American customs, but an immediate marriage would not, perhaps, be proper.

'It is a very serious matter, isn't it?' she went on. 'You do not know anything about me, my family . . . ' A little sadness touched her voice. 'Your love for me may not last, Mr Simpson. Perhaps you imagine it. A young man's love changes with the wind!'

She spoke simply and honestly. I tried hard to hide my grief. The next moment she pressed her hand in mine and smiled at me. She had forgotten, at once, all her reasons for *not* marrying me!

I said, 'Madam, my love for you will never change. It is

as strong as these great trees around us. To my eyes, your beauty will always be the same. I am ready to meet all the sweet problems that marriage brings. I hope that you will meet them with me – very soon.'

We went on talking for fifteen minutes. And at last she seemed willing to marry me, although something was still troubling her. I asked if she had any serious doubts.

'Yes, I have one,' she said. 'Perhaps you haven't thought about it – and a woman hates to discuss it!

'But there must be no secrets between *us*, Mr Simpson. I am thinking of our ages. Do you realise the difference between us? It doesn't matter if a gentleman is older than his wife. Indeed, he can be ten or even twenty years older, and that is quite all right. But I have always thought that a woman should never marry a *younger* man. It often causes unhappiness. Now – I know that you are twenty-two. I am older than that, Mr Simpson. Many – yes, many – years older.'

'My sweetest Eugenie,' I cried, 'who cares about that? Of course, you are older than I am. I have known it since I saw you first. But when people are in love – as we are – a year is only an hour! You say that I am twenty-two. That means that I shall soon be twenty-three. And you, my dearest, cannot be more than – more than – than – than – than – '

I expected her to tell me her age. But I had forgotten that she was French. Frenchwomen seldom give a direct answer to a personal question. They often think of a more practical reply. In my haste, I had almost said 'How old *are* you?'

A little ornament seemed to fall suddenly from the front

of her dress, and I picked it up. It was a very small picture in a round gold case. I gave it to her immediately.

'Keep it,' she said, smiling beautifully. 'Keep it for my sake. I am not as beautiful as that painting of me! Besides, on the back of it, you will find out what you want to know. It is too dark at present, of course, but you can look at it in the morning.

'And now, Mr Simpson, will you please take me home? My friends are having a musical party. If you would like to hear some good singing, please come into the house. I will try to hide you, or pretend that you are an old friend!'

She took my arm, and I walked home with her. It was a very big house and, I think, well furnished. It was not the custom, at that time, to light the lamps early. There was just one light in the largest room, and so I could not see clearly. The music had already started, and there were a lot of people there. Many of these were sitting in two other smaller rooms. Madame Lalande took me to a quiet corner in the second room, and sat down beside me.

It was the most wonderful evening of my life. The music and the singing were excellent – especially the singing of the ladies. We sat and listened for an hour, and I enjoyed every minute of it. Then there was a call: 'Madame Lalande! Madame Lalande, please!'

Eugenie stood up at once. A lady and two gentlemen came to our corner. I did not know the men. But the lady was the young woman I had seen with Madame Lalande at the theatre. The four of them went into the large room. I wanted to go with them, but felt doubtful about it: I did not know anyone there, except Madame Lalande, and she did not ask me to go. I decided to stay where I was.

I could not see Eugenie when she sang, but I heard her voice very clearly. It surprised me, I must say, but I did not know exactly *why*. What a voice! I have been to many theatres in Europe and America. I have heard most of the great singers. I do not think I have ever heard such a beautiful voice as Madame Lalande's. It was perfect, and – well, I need not say any more.

You are probably laughing about that. I loved her, of course, and so, naturally, I loved her voice as well. After she had sung three times, she came back to me, with stars in her eyes. I told her that I had been delighted. I did not say anything about my surprise, though, by then, I knew the reason for it. When she talked to me, her voice was never very strong. Once or twice it had seemed rather shaky, and I had not expected her to sing well.

We talked then for an hour or more. She asked me to tell her about my family and my life; and she listened with breathless attention to every word. I was as honest as she had been. I talked about my foolish amusements, my childish loves and quarrels, the illnesses that I had had. I explained my chief weakness – poor eye-sight. And, at the end, I begged her for a priceless favour. I asked her to marry me the next day.

She said, 'You told me about your eyes in your letter, and I felt very sorry. I should never have guessed – your eyes are such a beautiful grey. Why don't you wear glasses, Mr Simpson? If you need glasses, and don't wear them, you will make your sight worse. Sometimes I have to wear these – do you remember them?' She took from her bag the small pair of theatre-glasses.

'Oh yes!' I cried. 'I remember them very well, and they are very beautiful.'

'You see, if I move this little spring, they become a pair of ordinary spectacles. And this piece here – ' She touched the side of the glasses ' – makes them bigger or smaller.

'Well, then, Mr Simpson,' she went on, 'you have asked me to do something tomorrow. "A priceless favour" you called it. My heart has already agreed. If my lips agree too – will you do something as a favour to me?'

'Anything, Eugenie! Anything at all! Just ask! But – but I agree before you even ask.'

She said, 'For my sake, then, you must conquer your weakness. You must save your eye-sight before – before you get into serious trouble. I want you to wear these spectacles of mine. Ah, Mr Simpson – don't say anything! You have already agreed, haven't you?'

What could I say? I felt unhappy – *but what could I say?* Her wish was a condition of marriage. If I agreed to wear the glasses, she would marry me. If I did not agree – but I could not bear to think about that.

'Yes!' I cried. 'For your sake, I will do it! I will take the spectacles with me in my pocket. Tomorrow – but why not tonight, Eugenie? – we shall be married. At our first meal together – as husband and wife – I will put the spectacles on my nose. And after that, I will always wear them.'

We discussed then the arrangements for the wedding. Because it was so sudden, Eugenie wanted to keep it secret. 'In fact,' she said, 'I think you are right. It will be better if we get married tonight. This party will go on until two o'clock. If I leave the house with the visitors, no one is likely to notice . . . '

'Splendid!' I said. 'I don't want to waste a minute! I will go and bring a carriage for us.'

'Yes, we had better not use mine,' she said. 'But we shall have to warn the priest. I shall send my own servant –

I can depend on him – to the priest's house.'

'And then we will leave New York at once!' I cried. 'We will have a holiday on the coast!'

As soon as our plans were complete, I left the house. On the way to the carriage-station, I passed a hotel, with bright lights burning inside. I suddenly remembered the little picture of Eugenie in my pocket. I went into the hotel, put on the spectacles and looked at the ornament.

'Oh, she *is* beautiful!' I said to myself. 'Those large bright eyes! That proud and perfect nose! It is Eugenie exactly.' I turned the picture over and read the words – 'Eugenie Lalande, aged twenty-seven years and seven months.'

All our arrangements worked perfectly. Just after two o'clock in the morning, Madame Lalande and I arrived at the priest's house. The lady's servant was already there. The priest was a tall man, with a beard and a pair of thick spectacles. And so we were married.

At half past two, Madame Lalande and I – I mean Mrs Simpson and I – were driving out of New York. Three hours later, we stopped for a meal at an inn beside the road. I helped my dear wife out of the carriage and into the inn. I immediately ordered breakfast.

It was now daylight. I looked with love and pride at the beautiful woman by my side. It was, I think, the first time that I had been close to all that loveliness in daylight. I kissed her tenderly.

'And now, my dear,' she said, taking my hand, 'we are really and truly married. I have carried out my part of our agreement. I hope you have not forgotten yours. Ah, let me think. What was it? Yes, I remember. You promised to wear the spectacles at our first meal together – and after that, to wear them always.'

'My dearest,' I replied, 'any wish of yours is my delight. See! I have them ready – and I will wear them from this moment.'

As I was talking, Mrs Simpson sat up straight in her chair. She raised her cap a little, and then arranged her arms in front of her. I put the spectacles on my nose and turned to her. At once I felt the greatest surprise.

'My – my goodness!' I cried. 'My goodness! What *is* the matter with these glasses?' I took them off quickly and cleaned them with my handkerchief. Then I put them on again.

My first feeling had been the greatest surprise. My second was – *the greatest terror*! What did it mean? Were the glasses some kind of trick? Could I believe the – the things I saw? Was it red and white *powder* on my Eugenie's face? And were those – were those – were those *wrinkles* all over her face and neck? 'And oh gods and goddesses, tell me quick! – where are her teeth?' I threw the spectacles to the floor. I stood up. I raised my arms to heaven. My terror was so ugly that for a moment I could not talk.

Mrs Simpson looked straight into my face. 'Well, sir?' she asked. 'What is the matter with you? Are you ill? If you don't like me, why did you marry me?'

'You – you are evil!' I shouted. 'You – you miserable old woman!'

'Old woman? *Old*? No, no – I am not very old. I am only eighty-two.'

'Eighty-two!' I cried, falling back into my chair. 'Eighty-two hundred thousand monkeys! The picture said twenty-seven years and seven months!'

'It is true. I mean – it was true. Mr Lalande, my second husband, painted it when we were married. Only fifty-five years ago. Mr Lalande was a better artist than my first husband, Mr Moissart.'

'*Moissart*, madam?' I shouted. 'Did you say Moissart?'

'Yes, Moissart. What is the matter, sir?'

'My – oh, nothing, nothing. That name – Moissart!'

'That name?' she repeated. 'It's a very good name! And so is Voissart! My eldest daughter – Miss Moissart – she married Mr Victor Voissart. They are both very respectable names.'

'No – it can't be true! Not Moissart and Voissart!'

'And there are more, sir! My daughter's daughter – Miss Voissart – married Mr Croissart. And their daughter – Miss Marie Croissart – married Mr Charles Froissart, of Paris. They are all very respectable names. Not common names, like Simpson, sir!'

'*Froissart!*' I cried. I was ready to faint. 'Not Moissart, Voissart, Croissart and Froissart?'

'Yes,' she replied. 'Moissart, Voissart, Croissart and Froissart. But Mr Froissart was a great fool. He left France and came to this stupid America. We heard that he has a very stupid son, too – called Napoleon Froissart. But neither I nor my companion, Madame Julie Lalande, want to meet the young fool.'

By this time, Mrs Simpson was very angry indeed. She jumped up from her chair like a mad woman. She waved her arms in the air. She tore the cap from her head, and her hair – her wig! her beautiful black wig! – came off with it. She threw them both to the floor and danced on them angrily. Her own hair, thin and white, fell over her face.

'Moissart and Voissart,' I repeated thoughtfully, 'and Croissart and Froissart. And Napoleon Froissart!' I cried out, 'You devil! Napoleon Froissart – that's *me*! Do you hear? *It's me, me, me! I am Napoleon Froissart!* And I have married my great-great-grandmother!'

Eugenie Lalande – or should we say Mrs Simpson? – was indeed my great-great-grandmother. When she was young, she had been very, very beautiful. Even at the age of eighty-two, she was still tall and straight. Her eyes, her nose, the shape of her head, had not changed very much. With the help of powder and cream, false hair, false teeth and, of course, all the art of Paris, she still had beauty. The French call it 'past beauty'.

She was a very wealthy woman. Her second husband, Mr Lalande, and all her direct descendants were dead – except the son of Charles Froissart, in America. She had decided to look for him because she needed an heir. Her companion, the beautiful Madame Julie Lalande, was a distant relation of Eugenie's second husband. She was also a wealthy, but a young, widow.

At the theatre, my great-great-grandmother had noticed me watching her. When she examined me, through her glasses, she had a surprise. She thought that I looked very like Charles Froissart – my father – whom she remembered well.

She had then spoken to the gentleman with her. He told her that my name was Simpson – but had been Froissart. She thought immediately that I had discovered the family likeness in *her* face, and guessed who she was! And so she had smiled at me and bowed.

I remembered that I had questioned Talbot about her. He believed, naturally, that I was talking about the younger lady, Madame Julie. He replied truthfully that she was 'Madame Lalande, the most beautiful woman in New York . . . '

In the street, the next morning, my great-great-grandmother had met Talbot by chance. She had known him in Paris, several years before, and so they were old friends. They had talked about me, and Talbot had described my love for her! He blamed it on my weak eye-sight and my refusal to wear glasses.

Eugenie had been very angry at my stupidity – making love, in a theatre, to an old and unknown woman! She and Talbot had decided to punish me, to teach me a lesson. He pretended to be away from home. But in fact he had just moved to a friend's house not far away.

I had never seen Madame Eugenie closely and in daylight. At the party I had refused to put on the spectacles. It was, of course, the younger Madame Lalande who had sung so beautifully.

The 'priest' who had pretended to marry us was Talbot himself! The thick glasses he wore, and the false beard, deceived me completely.

I am very glad to say that I am *not* the husband of my great-great-grandmother. But I *am* the husband of Madame Lalande – Madame Julie Lalande. And when Eugenie dies – if she ever dies! – I shall be her heir. I have learned my lesson very well: I have never written another love letter; and no one in New York ever sees me *without* a pair of spectacles on my nose.

1 *'YOU ARE THE MAN'*

1 How was Mr Shuttleworthy going to travel to the city? 2 Who was Mr Shuttleworthy's closest friend?

1 What is *Château Margaux*? 2 How did Old Charley spend a good part of his time? 3 What had wounded Mr Shuttleworthy's horse?

1 What relation was Mr Pennifeather to Mr Shuttleworthy? 2 Why did Mr Pennifeather have few friends? 3 What had Mr Pennifeather once done to Old Charley?

1 What was Mr Pennifeather's plan for the search? 2 What kind of search did Old Charley advise? 3 What did the searchers find at the bottom of the pool?

1 What does an heir receive? 2 What did Mr Goodfellow find near the path?

1 What did Old Charley say would 'break his heart'? 2 What was Mr Shuttleworthy going to write?

1 Who found the shot in the horse's wound? 2 What was discovered about the shot? 3 What was the result of Mr Pennifeather's trial?

1 How did Mr Goodfellow repay people for their kindness to him? 2 Why did the letter surprise Old Charley?

1 At what time did the Château Margaux arrive? 2 Where did the people put the case of wine? 3 What did Old Charley confess?

1 Why had Mr Goodfellow killed Mr Shuttleworthy? 2 What happened to Mr Goodfellow when he stopped talking?

1 'That man never forgives and never forgets.' Whom does that sentence describe? 2 Where had Old Charley hidden Mr Shuttleworthy's body?

1 In what way was the body put into the box? 2 What happened to Mr Pennifeather?

2 *THE GOLD BUG*

1 Who was Jupiter? 2 On what did Legrand draw the bug? 3 What did I see when I looked at the drawing?

1 When did I visit Legrand next? 2 What did Legrand show me then? 3 What promise did Legrand make to me?

1 What was Legrand carrying when they left the hut? 2 What did Jupiter find on the seventh branch?

1 How did Legrand mark the spot where the gold bug fell? 2 Through which eye of the skull had Jupiter put the bug?

1 What was in the chest? 2 Where did they put the heavy things from the chest?

1 How did they carry home the heavy things? 2 What was the value of the coins in the chest? 3 How many gold watches were there?

1 What was the value of the whole treasure? 2 What had Jupiter used the parchment for?

1 What made the skull and cross bones appear on the parchment? 2 How had Captain Kidd written his name? 3 What happened when the ink dried?

1 In what language was the message written? 2 Which letter is used most often in that language?

1 How had Kidd written the word 'tree' in the message? 2 Who helped Legrand to find Bessop's Castle? 3 What was Bessop's Castle?

1 What was the meaning of the words 'a good glass'? 2 What did Legrand notice when he looked through the glass? 3 Who were the dead men who told no tales?

3 THE STOLEN LETTER

1 Who was Georges Godinot? 2 Why did the Princess want to hide the letter from the Countess Duval? 3 Who took the Princess's letter from the table?

1 *Complete this sentence*: The Princess knew that he had taken her letter. And he knew that.... 2 Why had the police attacked Lebrun?

1 What was Dupin's best advice to Georges? 2 How much money was Georges willing to pay for the letter?

1 When did Georges visit Dupin next? 2 *Complete this sentence*: Dupin said, 'Well, then, give me the money, and I will...'

1 *Complete, using one word only*: In Dupin's opinion, the police sometimes failed because they had no... 2 Why did Dupin wear dark glasses when he visited Lebrun? 3 What address was Lebrun trying to find?

1 *Complete this sentence*: Dupin said, 'The police never notice a thing just...' 2 What did Dupin leave on the table in Lebrun's house? 3 What made Lebrun run to the window and open it? 4 *Complete*: Dupin had promised to pay the man...if he...in the street outside Lebrun's house.

4 THE MURDERS IN THE RUE MORGUE

1 How did the policeman and the other men get into the house? 2 Which room was 'in terrible disorder'? 3 Where was Camille's body found? 4 How had Madame Espanaye been killed?

1 How many voices were heard? 2 What seemed strange about the high voice? 3 What did everyone notice about the windows?

1 Where did we see the two bodies? 2 *Complete this sentence*: 'Georges is

puzzled because these deaths are...' 3 Why did Dupin refuse to go for a walk?

1 What did we keep in our pockets? 2 What did Dupin think about the chimney as a way of escape? 3 How had the killer, or killers, escaped?

1 How were the windows kept shut? 2 What was wrong with the second nail? 3 *Complete the sentence*: The window had been shut with enough force to...

1 Dupin said, 'Think of the...terrible force that the killer used.' In what ways did the killer use terrible force? 2 Where had Dupin found the red-brown hairs? 3 What kind of hairs were they?

1 Why did Dupin hope that the animal was still free? 2 What was Dupin's address? 3 What did Dupin think about the piece of ribbon?

1 Had Dupin caught the orang-utan? 2 What 'payment' did Dupin ask for? 3 *Complete this sentence*: 'Lebon must be...' Dupin said.

1 Where had the sailor kept the animal? 2 How could the sailor see the inside of the room? 3 How did the orang-utan kill Camille Espanaye?

1 What happened to the orang-utan? 2 What did Georges Godinot think was 'unfair'?

5 DOWN INTO THE MAELSTROM

1 How old was the man? 2 What made him seem a lot older than that? 3 How far was the island of Moskoe from the shore?

1 Why did the rock shake? 2 For how long does the Maelstrom last? 3 For how long is the sea calm between the tides?

1 Why were there plenty of fish around those islands? 2 What happened to the man's younger brother? 3 Why did that not happen to the man himself?

1 The man's watch had stopped at seven o'clock. Did this fact make him more or less afraid? Why? 2 *Complete this sentence*: With the strength of a madman, my elder brother...

1 How far down had the ship immediately fallen? 2 What other things were travelling around the whirlpool? 3 Which things travelled fastest to the bottom of the whirlpool?

1 Which things might never reach the bottom? 2 '...the whirlpool began to change.' What were the changes? 3 Why did the man's friends not know him?

6 THE PIT AND THE PENDULUM

1 What was the man's punishment? (Give the answer in one word.) 2 Why was the man afraid to open his eyes? 3 What did he see when he did open them?

1 What did he find beside him when he woke? 2 Why did he almost faint with fear when he fell the second time? 3 What would have happened if he had not fallen?

1 How many pits were there in the room? 2 What had someone done to the man while he was sleeping? 3 What came out of the pit?

1 How far did the pendulum travel downwards during the first day? 2 What did the rats do while the man was sleeping? 3 Why would the knife never cut through the rope?

1 What did the man do with the last pieces of meat? 2 What happened to the rope? 3 How did the man know that someone was watching?

1 Why were the walls of the room coming together? 2 How was the man saved?

7 THE SPECTACLES

1 What did Napoleon Froissart have to do before he could receive the hundred thousand dollars? 2 What was Simpson's chief weakness?

1 Where did Simpson first see the lady? 2 Who was Simpson with when he saw her? 3 What is 'love at first sight'?

1 Where had Madame Lalande come from? 2 *Complete, using one word only*: Being a widow, she had no... 3 How did Madame Lalande examine Simpson?

1 Simpson felt 'ready for any madness'. What did he do? 2 Why did he feel as happy as any man could feel?

1 Where and when was Simpson going to meet Madame Lalande? 2 Why did he curse the whole family of Talbots? 3 'She is like a candle beside the evening star.' Who was 'like a candle'? Who was like the evening star?

1 How did Simpson discover Madame Lalande's address? 2 What offer did he make to her? 3 'Mr Simpson has guessed the truth.' What did Simpson think when he read that?

1 What advice did Talbot give Simpson? 2 What was Madame Lalande accustomed to doing in the evenings? 3 What was the cause of Simpson's grief?

1 '...and a woman hates to discuss it!' Madame Lalande said. What does a woman hate to discuss? 2 *Complete this sentence*: 'When people are in love, a year is...' 3 What did Madame Lalande tell Simpson to keep?

1 Why could not Simpson see the lady when she sang? 2 Why was he surprised when she sang? 3 What favour did Madame Lalande want?

1 Where did Madame Lalande send her servant? 2 Where was Simpson when he examined the little painting? 3 At what time was the marriage?

1 How old was the lady? 2 How old was the little painting? 3 What was the lady wearing on her head?

1 What relation was Eugenie to Simpson? 2 What helped Eugenie to look beautiful? 3 Who was Madame Julie? 4 Why had Eugenie smiled at Simpson in the theatre? 5 Why had Eugenie and Talbot decided to punish Simpson? 6 What lesson did Simpson learn?

PRONOUNCING THE NAMES

The symbols are those of the Simplified International Phonetic Alphabet, as used in Michael West's *International Reader's Dictionary* (Longman).

Barnabas Shuttleworthy	'ba:nəbəs 'ʃʌtlwə:ði
Charley	'tʃa:li
Jupiter	'dzu:pitə
Lofoten	ləu'fəutən
Maelstrom	'meilstrəum
Pennifeather	'penifeoə
Rattleborough	'ratlbərə
Simpson	'simsn

French names should have their French pronunciation, or in certain cases an English form that is given here:

Camille	ka'mi:l	Musset	'musei
Espanaye	'espanei	Paris	'paris
Froissart	'frwʌsa:	Rue Genève	ru: ə'nev
Godinot	'godinəu	Rue Morgue	ru: 'mo:g
Lalande	la'lond		

LIST OF EXTRA WORDS

Barrel	Mud
Box (theatre)	Nephew
Bug	Orang-utan
Cards (play)	Parchment
Castle	Pendulum
Cloth	Pirate
Confess/ion	Pit
Countess	Pool
Degree (compass)	Relation
Diamond	Ribbon
Ditch	Sack
Dozen	Sash (window)
False	Skull
Franc	Spade
Guilty	Spectacles
Habit	Tale
Handful	Telescope
Heir	Throat
Holder (letter-)	Tide
Initial (n.)	Tool
Invite	Waistcoat
Leather	Whirlpool
Maelstrom	Widow
Main	Wig
Miracle	Will (money)